TAKING THE DEVIL'S ADVICE

Anne Fine

ISIS

First published in Great Britain 1990
by Viking

Published in Large Print 2000 by ISIS Publishing Ltd,
7 Centremead, Osney Mead, Oxford OX2 0ES, and
ISIS Publishing, PO Box 195758,
Winter Springs, Florida 32719-5758, USA
by arrangement with David Higham Associates

British Library Cataloguing in Publication Data
Fine, Anne, 1947-
    Taking the devil's advice. – Large print ed.
    1. Black humour (Literature) 2. Large type books
    I. Title
    823.9'14[F]

ISBN 0-7531-6287-3 (hb)
ISBN 0-7531-6288-1 (pb)

Printed and bound by Antony Rowe, Chippenham and Reading

For Tik Enif

ACKNOWLEDGEMENT

I am indebted to my good friend
Linda Robinson Walker,
and to her writing

The Devil's Advice to Storytellers

. . . my advice to storytellers is
Weigh out no gross of probabilities,
Nor yet make diligent transcriptions of
Known instances of virtue, crime or love,
To forge a picture that will pass for true,
Do conscientiously what liars do —
Born liars, not the lesser sort that raid
The mouths of others for their stock in trade:
Assemble, first, all casual bits and scraps
That may shake down into a world perhaps . . .
Sigh then, or frown, but leave (as in despair)
Motive and end and moral in the air;
Nice contradiction between fact and fact
Will make the whole read human and exact.

Robert Graves

CHAPTER
ONE

Look at this. Look! What a *cheek*. Look what I've found hidden away at the back of the bloody airing cupboard.

She has been writing in my autobiography again. She so annoys me. Why must she poke her nose in everything, meddling and prying, forever insisting on her right to be taken into account? Sometimes I think my last few waking hours of Perfect Privacy must have passed by, unnoticed and unvalued, the day before I met Constance. How long is it since we parted — three years? Four? Yet here she is, snooping around my room whenever I'm out, leafing through papers on my table, reading the (few) bits that interest her and scribbling her irritating little comments and additions down the margins and over on the back. I can't put up with this for three more months. I should never have agreed to spend the summer here in the first place. It was a foolish idea, and I'm not sure it's even very good for the children. I'll have to move out and find somewhere else. Or buy a large tin box with a good lock.

And yet, let's face it, I'm not here by accident, am I? I did choose of my own free will not to spurn Constance's offer of a place to stay, and I can't argue that I didn't live with her long enough to know exactly what she's like. I must have realized Constance could no more stay peacefully and incuriously outside a room in which her former husband is writing anything of a remotely personal nature than she could fly unaided to the moon. I must have known that she'd be in and out all the time, rooting through, checking, complaining, criticizing; that even the most casual attempt to pin down a few simple dates would turn one mealtime after another into great atavistic wrangles about the reasons for this move, that baby, those blinding arguments; that it would be three months of pure hell. It isn't even as if what Constance remembers is of any relevance. I'm not writing that sort of autobiography, and, if I were, this is the last place on earth I'd choose to write it. I'm here because all my philosophical papers are still in the attic. Why else would I suffer the indignity of living and sleeping up in my old study while this great shambling amiable Ally sleeps in my old bed with my old wife?

But I might have known from the start that it wouldn't work out. You only have to mention the past to Constance and she's in there like a blowtorch, scorching away all your precious layers of self-protection until there's nothing left of you. Then she stamps on your shadow. The trouble with Constance, of course, is that she's ruthless. Look at this. Look what she's written here. I gave what I thought was a perfectly honest and accurate assessment of the two years I spent at Nitshill Road County Infant School. "Of my time there," I wrote, "I can remember practically nothing." And in the margin she's printed, spitefully and neatly: "Oh yes you can.

2

Don't you remember telling me about that time you were accused of looking up at the girls' knickers, playing hopscotch?"

Well, thank you, Constance. Yes, I do remember now. I remember the sudden bitter taste in my mouth and the rushes of desperation and of hate, and wanting to poke out the eyes of everyone standing round jeering and pointing. Why did they take such prompt advantage of the opportunity to laugh at me? Was it because we were poor and my clothes were so shabby? Was it because my mum was fat? Was it because, behind the fungus of his Jewish beard, my father looked like a bit of a nutter? Yes, it's all flooding back now, thank you, Constance, as clearly as if it were yesterday. Once again I feel quite sick with the embarrassment and shock and shame. My heart is actually thumping inside me. It'll take me a couple of minutes to calm down. And it doesn't help to know that, by the time I finally pull myself together sufficiently to take my place at the supper table, Ally and the children will be peering curiously and sympathetically at me — fresh from the entertainment of Constance's "Honestly, it's *true*" account of something I confided to her once and once only, in bed, deep in the healing and forgiving dark, and then forgot again for twenty years.

"*Forgot*? How could you possibly forget something like that?"

I'm always having to defend myself, even from my own children. Bonnie, especially, leans across the table ready to pounce. She's getting dangerously like her mother.

"I just did. I forgot, all right? Not everyone remembers exactly the same sort of things about their very early schooling."

"What sort of things do you remember?"

"All sorts of things."

"Don't get all huffy. Tell us. We want to know. What sort of things do you remember?"

"Oh, this is misery. Even kind Alasdair, who tires so easily of watching torture, is peering with interest over the salad bowl. He wants to know what I remember too.

"Very well, then. I can remember — pegs."

"What?"

"Pegs."

"*Pegs*?"

"Pegs, yes. You've heard the word, I take it. Pegs."

"What sort of pegs?"

"All sorts of pegs." I'm getting irritable with Bonnie now. "I had a little lamb peg in the infant school, I remember. And a blue one with a big fat knob on the end in the juniors. They were all the same at the Grammar, of course: black, with a double hook." They're watching me now, the whole lot of them: Ally with sympathy, Constance and Bonnie like the pair of ghouls they are, and Nance with innocent curiosity. I turn to Nance. "Sometimes, if you were sick on the first day, or yours was an especially large class, you had to share."

There's a long wait, then Constance asks sweetly:

"How about shoe-bags, Oliver? How is your memory for shoe-bags?"

When did this paranoia first set in? Ten years ago? Fifteen? Not at the start, surely. When we first met I was thrilled, I remember, if a bit confused, to have such interest taken in me. I thoroughly enjoyed Constance's persistent, soft, baffling inquisitions. No-one at home had ever paid the slightest attention to anything I said or thought or did, unless they thought that they could pick a hole in it. In our house you would have had to have blown the roof off to turn more than a couple of heads in your direction for more than a couple of seconds. Oh, how I hated it! The pandemonium. Great, grinding arguments. More than a quarter of a lifetime spent elbowing for larger helpings of food, first go in the lavatory, more access to the rickety one-barred fire. (The din must have been prodigious. We didn't have carpets.) Now I glance over the table at my own hothouse offspring, and my childhood strikes me in retrospect as quite extraordinary, as if I'd been raised in a sort of rugby scrum. But at the time, and for years afterwards, I assumed that it must have been perfectly normal. Indeed, the first time I remember having doubts was after an exchange with Bonnie when she was much the same age Nance is now, and driving me mad with her tireless fidgets.

"Can't you go in the garden?"

"I've *been* in the garden."

The sheer bloody privilege of it took my breath away. And in a flash I was back, pint-sized, in that scuffed and miserable pocket-handkerchief pen, frantically rattling the door knob. What was I snivelling about this time? Torn knees? Frozen fingers? What difference did it make? I can still hear the half-demented shriek through the kitchen window: "You can't come in yet! It's not dinner time."

Did I tell Constance? It would have made one of those juicy little titbits that go to feed a living marriage: "I had a really peculiar memory this morning. I'd just told Bonnie to go out in the garden . . ." Or did I keep it to myself? When did I first become suspicious of Constance and her continual interest in me? There must have been some sort of watershed in our marriage, some period of steadily burgeoning distrust, as I came to believe that, though she still listened to the things I told her, it was no longer in good faith in order to learn more about me and understand better, but rather, like some police sleuth on the trail of inconsistency or weakness, simply in order to be able to shout "Gotcha!"

I'm not afraid of Constance. I never have been.

"Shoe-bags? Oh, *shoe*-bags. Well, let me see. I do remember that it was always in my school shoe-bag that I hid the money I stole to buy chips."

Now that's pricked up old Ally's ears.

"Stole money to buy chips? Where from?"

"From the chip shop, of course."

(He asks for it, really he does.)

"But I thought . . ."

He can't quite bring himself to come out with it, but he's looking puzzled. No doubt Constance has held forth freely and often about what a frightful strain it was, living with such a stubborn pillar of rectitude. I bet she's even told him about that time I tore up the duplicated rebate from the Gas Board.

"You thought, Ally . . . ?"

(I really shouldn't tease him. It isn't nice.)

"Well, you know . . . Stealing . . ."

"We were hungry, Alasdair. *Hungry*."

We were too. It took me years and years to get out of the
habit of gobbling food. Even now, in a smart restaurant
and in smart company, I'll still unthinkingly pick up tiny
scraps of food that have slid off the edge of my plate
from the tablecloth, and nibble them. Solly claimed
there were actually times we counted the baked beans
off the serving spoon on to the slices of toast; and though
I can't quite believe it, it could be true. Certainly I can
remember her opening that battered green purse of hers
and screaming at him: "See! It's empty! Empty! *Empty*!"
and him turning away as he always did when she began
to raise her voice at him, as if his personal code of
chivalry demanded that a husband should avert his eyes
from a woman reduced to fishwife screeching.

I didn't mind her screeching. I minded her weeping.
What I couldn't bear was seeing her sprawled on the
cracking lino, snivelling in temporary defeat. Better the
ugly sobbing that came with her rages, when she'd go
reeling round the room beating the walls with her fists
until you feared the bones in them would crack, hissing,
"I hate him! I hate him! I hate him!"

It wasn't his fault. The two of them should never have
married, everyone's agreed on that. And it's not as if
their families didn't warn them. Far from it. Apparently
on both sides it was an issue. Was that why the Rosens
and the Solomons kept their distance so assiduously
throughout our childhood — because their sound advice
had been ignored? I can remember hardly anything

about my relations. No, that's not true. I have a host of memories: hating to kiss Granny Ruth's downy cheeks; musty drapes darkening the Ealing parlour; Uncle Joe's crippled signature across the bottom of each flowery birthday card; the time his tortoise — oh, bugger it. Who cares? Let the whole pack rot unremembered in their selfish graves. It's not enough to club together and buy a house so huge and tumbledown no-one else wants it, then smugly wipe your hands of the whole sorry boiling, saying, "Well, we've done our bit. You're on your own now." Where were they the years he couldn't hold down a job, the months on end he was away "in hospital, trying to get better", the week their one and only girl baby lived and died? Where were they the morning I found her weeping on the steps because she'd left a loaf on a shop counter? One miserable loaf, for heaven's sake. Two slices each? Why, I've seen Constance heave out entire breadbinfuls without a second thought: "Whoops! How long's this lot been here? Is that mould?"

Funny, it's always her feelings I remember, never his. Is that because, even in those days, I was already hostile? Certainly I can't remember a time when he and I didn't get along badly. My vision of him, as far back as it goes, is of an intruder, an obstructionist, a spoiler. Had you managed, somewhere in that vast, echoing, unfurnished box, to find yourself a peaceful corner? He'd seek you out and find you a little job to do. Had you suddenly discovered you could pick out all the tunes you knew with no trouble at all on Sol's school recorder? He needed absolute quiet in order to think.

Had she let you (just for a couple of minutes, Olly, mind) into the haven of her soft warm bed? "Better not let him. It will just set a precedent." Well, there's two ways of looking at that, isn't there? What was that flowery old proverb Constance's mother was forever quoting when she was urging Constance to ignore all my doubts, and go ahead with starting another baby? "The more angels, the more room for them." Now I can't claim to feel all that easygoing about serial procreation myself. I reckon, all things taken into account, each of our two burned a good three years off my effective working life. But nonetheless, there is a point to be made here. It should be possible, if you have several, not deliberately to limit to a strict fraction the love and care you give to each.

And why have so many in the first place? It's not as if they were daft. The more I wonder why I was born at all (having no precedence, being the fourth), the more I think that Constance might be right, though when she first came out with the theory I practically bit her head off. It seemed, with my mother no longer above ground to confirm or deny it, such a pointless and somehow offensive assertion: "I reckon she only bothered to have all you lot in the first place to keep your dad off her for a bit." But when we cleared the house after his funeral, I found that book again — the book he'd handed so shyly to vast, blooming Constance all those years before. I flicked through, despising my own prurience, and there it was, the passage he'd marked for her in soft, blunt pencil: "All intercourse in pregnancy should be strictly avoided," followed by half a page of unscientific drivel

9

about how a woman's blood vessels contract in orgasm, cutting the oxygen supply to the foetal brain.

Finn came across to tick me off for wasting precious time, and I raised the book with the marked paragraph. Finn was amused. "My God!" He strolled back, chuckling, to the piles of obsolete coins he was tipping from the roll-top desk into a Sainsbury's carrier bag. "If that's true, my two should have turned out to be morons!"

Too right. And mine. And how did he go without it for nine whole months, anyway? I don't think I could have stood it — not in the same bed. Perhaps he didn't have a choice. Perhaps, whenever he reached out for her, she jackknifed up, raising her hand like a traffic cop: "No, Leonard, no! Think of its faculties!" Or maybe it was he who played the monk, forced on by fierce conscience and just a fraction of uncertainty. He must have wanted her. He was like me. (Don't ask me how I know. I just do. I only have to glance at a photograph, or conjure him up again in my mind's eye, and I know for certain that, in this respect at least, we are alike.) It must have been murder, and it shows true grit that he presumably held out through each interminable pregnancy (not like poor Constance's pathetic efforts to give up cigarettes when she was expecting). But then my family is obsessed with brains, a fact of life, take it however you want — how Constance used to take it, cheerful and cajoling: "Oh, come now, Olly. You only have to look around to see that brains don't make you any happier!" How she takes it now: "For God's sake, Oliver! Is it *genetic*, rating happiness so low?"

10

"Is what genetic?"

"Beg your pardon?"

"You just leaned across the table and snarled: 'Is it genetic?'"

"Did I? Oh, sorry."

"No need to apologize," says Constance. "I don't *mind*. I was just curious. I was just wondering what on earth you were thinking."

(Oh, ho. The Thought Police. Take care now, Oliver.)

"I was just thinking about my earliest memories."

"Oh, yes? More pegs?"

"Pegs?"

"Be careful," Constance warns, spooning out macaroni. "Forget the pegs, and you'll have no earliest memories at all."

Bonnie's there in a flash. "Of course he will. Either Dad has no memories at all, or he has only one memory, or he must have an earliest memory. What about the time he hid under that bush in the park and shaved his legs because he thought that was the only way he could save himself from growing up as hairy as Grandpa Leonard, and he was seen and everyone laughed at him? Or that time he was so pleased to be invited to a birthday party for once, and he ate so many cakes and jellies he was sick, and they all laughed at him? Or that time he stole money from his mum's purse to buy a box of Black Magic for the girl in the next desk because he'd got a giant crush on her, and she gave one to everybody in the class except him, and they all laughed at him?"

"Don't!" Constance stops her. "Don't, Bonnie! I can't bear it!"

You can see why, with Constance, I was a winner from the start. I think it must be the main reason she married me, because I had a seemingly inexhaustible fund of Tales from a Miserable Childhood. (I see she's touched them up and passed them on.) It wasn't deliberate on my part, trawling for sympathy. She asked the questions, I just answered them. How was I to know that Constance was, both by inclination and training, a sort of reconstruction expert? She takes after her mother, the Salvage Queen. I only have to hear my mother-in-law's name now, and I get this vision of her sailing through the door, handing her suitcase to me as if the only reason I'm standing there is to take it from her, and scooping up one or another of the children.

"*Aren't* you a little poppet? Aren't you smashing? Haven't you *grown*? Let me just button you up a bit better, there's a little angel. Did you have a nice chukky egg for breakfast? Yes, I can see that you did. I can see it on your face" (rub rub) "and your rompers" (scratch, scratch) "and your ears" (tweak, tweak) "and your elbow" (spit on hanky, polish, polish). "There. That's better, isn't it? Doesn't that feel better? Of course it does. Now, would you like to see what I've got for you? Of course you would. There. Isn't that lovely? A little brown horse. You've always wanted a little brown horse, haven't you? See the rider? Hasn't she got a nice hat on? Clippety-clop. Clippety-clop. No, not on the table. We don't gallop horses along the nice table top, do

12

we? Here's a nice rug. Make the nice horsie gallop along Mummy's grubby old rug. Did you buy any of that carpet cleaner I told you about, Constance? Can't you get it round here?"

There was no-one like that in our house. No-one to scoop you up and dust you off and send you, sorted out, on your way. And no-one to take up battle on behalf of nice table tops, either. Our house fell steadily apart at the seams. Never far up in line for a Good Housekeeping Award, my mother withdrew further and further into Great Russian Novels while the huge lumps of ugly auction furniture stood starkly abandoned round bare walls, shelves fell, cupboards spilled open, ash buckets overflowed. My father, by his lights, made one or two efforts: "Take your feet off the rungs of that chair." "Whoever is dropping apple cores in the lavatory is to stop it!" But basically he was more taken with the fault-finding than with the outcome. Who'd go to the trouble of sprucing up a battleground between such regular engagements?

And that's all the house was really, a battleground — firing lines sharply drawn. Some couples mark their flannels "his" and "hers". They marked their children. Finn, Gerry and Lou were his, Solly and Joe and myself were hers. (I was her favourite, I think; but that wasn't, in the general context, of much significance.) The divisions were known and accepted, and even referred to openly in argument: "Of course she'd say that. You are one of hers!" I'm not sure what it was like to be one of his, but I remember only too well what it meant not to be: suffering his endless, grinding criticism; having to stand and listen while he came out with spurious justifications for each of his small meannesses; and, worst of all, knowing that whatever your triumphs and achievements he would maintain a determined indifference. Is it surprising that I loved my mother? She may not have been the most attentive and caring of parents. I dare say in the general run of things she would rate pretty low. But still I can't forget that she did try to defend me against some of his more impossible embargoes and rulings. I think she came close to braining him with the iron lampstand that night he told me I could keep practising the piano all right, but I must stop pressing down the keys! It was she who found me that piano, a monstrous battered thing she bought for five pounds at a local auction. And she pitched out on wet nights to come to my concerts. She tried to support me, and I remember her with warmth and gratitude as well as love; indeed, the first time I remember feeling the stirrings of real hatred for Constance was when I caught her sneakily trying to throw out the shiny brown vinyl suitcase my mother scrimped to buy so I could go on Youth Music Week without the embarrassment of carrier bags — probably one of the only occasions on which Constance's sensitivities (concerning, in this case, cheap plastic luggage) have been entirely matched by my own. She did her best, my mother, as long as she could, and I can't find it in my heart to blame her for giving up so easily. Sol says she should have made more of an effort to stay alive, if only for Joe's sake — swears he remembers watching her drop a letter from the hospital consultant into the rubbish bin. Maybe. I can't judge. All I know is, in her position, I would have slit my throat ten years before, not waited for the cancer to get me.

After she died, he got along surprisingly well, considering. Oh, he was mad. (She wasn't really dead, but being kept alive in some Swiss sanatorium while they experimented with her body; the Council may call it fluoride, but it was actually something far more sinister; there was something wrong with the way Solly washed up the dishes. He didn't want to go into it. He didn't want to explain. He just didn't want Solly washing up dishes.) But, on the whole, the six of us took singularly little notice. There were huge areas of inconvenience, of course. He couldn't bear strangers coming to the house, and wouldn't let Sol install a telephone on the (unarguable) grounds that people might be tempted to phone us up. But I can't claim that any of it really bothered me. After my mother's death, he somehow didn't seem to matter any more. Overnight he became little more than a prowling irritation. Each time he picked me up for some petty misdemeanour I realized with renewed vigour just how much I disliked him; but that was about the limit of it. And, in some ways, life was a whole lot easier. For one thing, for the first time in years and years he managed to find, and keep, a reasonable job (biking in and out scrupulously one hour late for half the year, of course, since he stayed on Greenwich Mean Time on principle). Then, too, he seemed less combative overall, now that his only serious adversary had folded her tent and disappeared. He spent a lot of his time, I remember, writing to toffee manufacturers, asking for detailed lists of their ingredients. And he had his fatherly moments. Lou can recount, word for word, a bedtime story of impenetrable plot featuring aniseed balls with which he was, he claims, calmed to sleep night after night. He brought home licorice bootlaces (long after we'd moved on to cigarettes). He sponsored Gerry's cow in Botswana. He fixed my bike.

And we grew up. We made it. We're all big and strong and healthy — well, Solly's dead, of course, and I can't speak for Joe because he's disappeared, but he was big and strong before he vanished. Constance's family might raise their eyebrows when I claim that, all things considered, we did all right; but, let's face it, poor Constance can't go on a day trip to Boulogne without phoning everyone to make sure they remember what's to happen to the children if her boat sinks. (It wouldn't surprise me if the reason our lawyer moved into a larger office was to make room for all Constance's notes.) The trouble with Constance is, because she's sunk so much of her own life into being a mother, she doesn't seem to realize that you can suffer from the worst of parenting, and still grow up. We did. All of us sailed through school, for example. We might have been scruffy, but we weren't thick. And we were, by and large, left alone — at least, I know I was. I spent hours in that tiny stationery cupboard under the fire stairs in a top maths set of my own, forging my way through whole series of textbooks. I think I was perfectly happy. What more could I have wanted? I had an established fantasy that, only if I successfully broke the mathematical code with which I was struggling, would my beloved home planet be saved. (I was Revilo Nesor, King of Mars.) I had milk at breaktime, and a filling lunch. (I loved school dinners. I'd face the barracking to go up to the hatch for thirds.) The building was warm, and, in its own way, comfortable. And, best of all, school was a good four miles from home.

Home. The very thought of it still makes me shudder. What did I do, for heaven's sake, before the Great and Glorious Escape? Well, I must have spent weeks on end at that piano, driving them mad with Scarlatti and Liszt, Tchaikovsky and Schubert, Mussorgsky and Chopin — whichever passion of the moment was helping the days pass. And sometimes I came out and joined in the arguments. They used up hours. Oh, God, did they use up the hours! In our house, an argument about two leftover prunes could mean an afternoon of solid wrangling. We must have been indefatigable. It never stopped, the table-thumping, the interrupting, the heads poking round doorways to make fresh points or yell support for others yelling even louder. Come evening we'd still be wandering in and out of rooms after one another, disputing premises, pointing out fallacies, dismissing irrelevancies, questioning conclusions. No wonder I'm a bloody philosopher. Someone like Constance wouldn't have lasted five minutes in our house. Look at her, pushing out the plate of blackcurrant tart she's just cut so carefully and neatly into five.

"I think that's fair."

Fair? What's *fair*? Fair by age? Body weight? Labour contributed? Fair on simple utilitarian grounds, side-stepping any considerations of justice (in which case Nance should have the lot because she loves it so)? At 73 Nitshill Road, a careless remark like that would have led to a riot. Here, Constance can announce she thinks something's fair, and everyone murmurs their happy agreement! I'm used to it now, of course; but, at the start, it struck me as being downright unnatural.

Mind you, they're not a great family for promoting abstract thought, the Taylors. I'll not forget that time Bonnie was sitting on the lavatory swinging her legs while I was shaving. How old was she? Three? Four at the very most. And out she came with it, just like that:

"How do I know that all this round me isn't just a dream?"

Before I even realized that I'd nicked myself with the razor, mother-in-law had stepped in.

"Don't be so silly, Bonbons. Wipe your bum."

Can you believe it? To the philosopher's daughter! I was quite sharp. Constance and I had a blazing row afterwards, about the tone I took with her mother. I bet no-one even remembers now.

"Bonnie, do you recall, when you were very young indeed, wondering how you could ever be quite sure that everything around you wasn't a dream?"

"No. Sorry."

Constance is there in a flash, of course, taking the piss.

"What about you, Nance? Ever thought we might just be shadows flickering on a cave wall?"

Nance's spoon drifts to a halt midway between her plate and her mouth. She looks confused.

"No?" Constance leans closer. "Well, what about worrying whether, if there's a tree in the quad that no-one ever sees but God, it's really there at all?"

Nance's troubled look clears.

"I think, if it was worrying me, I'd probably go and have a look."

Constance shrugs.

"Never mind, Olly. They are both yours, I promise you."

I don't care if it does upset poor Alasdair. I'm batting back.

"Constance! I'd no idea that, somewhere along the long stony path of our marriage, you'd picked up so many little nuggets. What a pity you have absolutely no notion of their value."

Glad I'm not that piece of blackcurrant tart that she's stabbing.

"Don't go all snotty on me, Oliver. You can't complain when I tease about philosophy. You're quick enough to sneer at what other people do all day long!"

Ally's already leaning back in his seat and reaching up to the top of the fridge, where Nance, under orders, left her large bag of popcorn before the meal. "Do you mind finishing it outside, Nance? I just swept the floor."

Gratefully, peace-loving Nance slips off her chair and disappears. But Bonnie's staying, it appears, fully plugged in. She takes an unhealthy interest in arguments between me and her mother.

"I don't believe I sneer at what other people do, Constance."

"Oh, no? What about yesterday, when I was in here having a chat with Ned about not telling any more lies to me or his father? What did you say as you went by?"

Ally's torn now, I can tell. Part of him wants to break this up right away, but part of him wants to know what I said. Ned is his own son, after all.

It's too late, anyway. Constance is after blood.

"Well, Oliver? What did you say?"

"Not sure I can remember, exactly."

"I can. I can remember perfectly well. You heard me telling Ned that lying is wrong, and you couldn't butt in fast enough. 'Sometimes it might be right to tell a lie,' you said. 'Suppose a man burst through that door with froth dripping from his lips, swirling a bloodstained hatchet round his head, asking for Ally. You wouldn't say your dad was standing in the shower, stark naked, with soap in his eyes, would you? You'd tell the maniac that he'd gone down to the shops.'"

It's a pretty good imitation. I can actually sense Ally keeping his face straight. But now she drops it, and leans angrily across the table. "I'm trying to teach a small child right from wrong." She snaps her fingers in my face. "And *that's* how much respect you have!"

Ah.

"I may have found myself recoiling a little from the proposition that lying was always totally morally indefensible. I'm sure I never said all that."

"You did!"

"I didn't."

"Yes, you did!"

TIME!

Ally is on his feet.

"Blimey!" he says, hastily stacking dishes. "I'd no idea philosophy was so exciting. Pass your plate, Constance. Is that what all those weighty tomes in your room are full of, Oliver? Nutters with frothing lips and bloodstained hatchets?"

Oh, fair enough. He did cook half the meal, after all. It's not right to ruin the whole of lunchtime.

"Well, not exactly, Alasdair. But a lot of philosophers do pride themselves on their colourful examples."

"Can't pride themselves on their colourful lives," Constance mutters spitefully. "Pack of inadequates."

The trouble with Constance, of course, is that she never knows when to stop. To be quite fair, I think it's probably more a matter of well-primed sources of adrenalin than any deliberate sabotage of poor Ally's careful peacekeeping procedures. But still, it takes its toll. He does have to work harder.

"Are there a lot of these odd little philosophical examples, then, Oliver?"

"Dozens. Hundreds, probably." Oh, hell. He swept the floor, too, after all. Better give him a hand. "I'll tell you the one that used to drive poor Constance demented. It's called The Ship of Theseus."

"The Ship of Theseus. I'd forgotten that!" Her eyes flash, and she's off. We can relax. "I tell you, Ally, it is the stupidest problem you ever heard! And they spent hours on it! Days! Weeks! Years!"

(I could murmur "Lifetimes!" at her, but she's not listening.)

"There's this ship. It belongs to Theseus, and so it's called The Ship of Theseus."

"That follows," Ally says. (He sounds relieved.)

"It gets more and more tatty as time goes by, so every now and again the sailors heave a rotting plank overboard, and fit in another."

"Makes sense." (He sounds surprised. Does he imagine that we professional philosophers live in a dream world?)

"Gradually, over the years, every single plank in the ship gets replaced. Every last one. And — this is the good bit, Ally — all the old planks just happen to float away in the same direction, and fetch up, one by one, on the very same island."

He's leaning back in his chair now, enjoying the story. I can tell that he's getting just a tiny bit complacent.

"Now," Constance carries on. "On this island it just so happens that there's a master shipbuilder, marooned. So he collects the planks as they wash up on his beach, and, one day, when he thinks he's got enough, he sets to and builds himself a ship. And it just so happens — pure coincidence, you understand — that every single rotting plank ends up exactly in its very own place!"

Bonnie's got it, I'm interested to see. Her face is already crumpling up with thought. But Ally's still looking delicately interested. He's not sure whether that's the end or not.

"Well? Don't you see? Which is The Ship of Theseus?"

"Which?"

Oh, God. I can't believe he's floundering. Surely not.

"Yes. Which? Is it the old one — I mean the one that's just been rebuilt from all the old planks? Or is it the new one that Theseus is sailing about in?"

There's a long silence. Then he turns to me.

"Is that it? Is that really the sort of thing that you philosophers think about for a living?"

I don't get the chance to explain. Constance is already in there, crowing.

"That's it! That's what they do! And they get paid. By taxpayers! You and me! Well, you anyway. Well, not even you this year since you didn't earn enough again. But if you had —"

It's quite amazing. She's perfectly cheered up. She's so mercurial. I've never understood the way her mood can swing within moments from semi-pathological rage to easy merriment. I could break in now and explain to Ally that, though he would never guess it from this tricksy little example, the Problem of Identity — in what, exactly, is identity invested — has always been one of the Great Central Questions of Western Philosophy. But what's the point? It would only irritate Constance, and she's in such a good mood now — well away on one of the more broken-backed of the Taylor family hobby horses: the sheer uselessness of knowledge for its own pure sake. How did I ever come to marry someone like her? She is an intellectual Luddite. I must have noticed from the start. How come it didn't seem to matter?

Oh, be honest, Oliver. You know the answer well enough. It's staring you in the face. In many ways you actually liked it. Seems hard to credit now it drives you mad, but back in the old days Constance must have appeared to you much as she does to Alasdair now: witty, attractive, amusing, different. She was a break from seriousness, a rest from thought. Look at her, enchanting gullible Ally with further examples of what she claims to be philosophical idiocies, leaping sure-footedly from one garbled travesty to another. (I really should stop Bonnie listening.) Her face is lit, she's quite unbelievably happy, and she's talking so fast poor Ally can barely follow the words she's saying, let alone their mangled substance or their ill-informed drift. Not that he's even listening, probably. You can tell from the expression on his face that he's just sitting there drinking her in, adoring her good spirits and her loquacity. He's probably fancying her a bit, as well. I know I used to, especially after lunch. She's always more fun in the afternoons. But we're not married any longer. It's not my job to step in and stop her pouring out these frightful misrepresentations and distortions. What do I care if Ally never understands why I'll spend my whole life doing philosophy; never knows why, for me, these are immense and awesome and towering questions; why one lifetime could not possibly offer a fraction of the time I need to understand the way I want to understand; why, for me, years go by as if I'd only blinked, and I'm still thinking about the very same problems, only deeper, far deeper. It's all right for people like Constance. They're free. Someone like her can fall about, convulsed, at the lunch table, playing cheap little philosophical parlour games to amuse her new lover. Go ahead, Constance. But some of us are shackled for life. I stand with

Theseus on his firm new deck in a good wind, seeing, to his astonishment, a ship sail past, and wondering with him: "Which ship is mine?" (Neither? Both? This one? That one? *Why*? Perhaps that one first, but, at a certain point, this one — or vice versa. But at which point? And why? Why? *Why*?)

At least the meal is over, thank God. And here it comes, as usual. Constance's idea of a Great Central Question:

"Whose turn is it to load the dishwasher? Is it yours, Olly?"

CHAPTER
TWO

He's an ungrateful shit, you know, biting the hands that spend half their lives feeding him. I've just found more. I've just found another whole pile stuffed in a Victoria Plum pillowcase. It carries on.

Who's writing this autobiography anyway, that's what I'd like to know. This morning, in great good spirits, I finally finished my chapter on Oxford. I gave a pretty full account, I thought, of those of my tutors who still stick in the memory. I described my rooms in college, inasmuch as I can remember a thing about them. And I even tried little pen-sketches of both my friends — Tanny, a rather shy older man from Taiwan, and Silas Allardyce, a skittish High Anglican of my own age, known round the college as much for his rather trying periods of remorse as for his periodic bouts of quarrelsomeness. Admittedly I didn't go mad over either of these descriptions — I can see, looking back, that the three of us weren't actually all that close, and I wanted to get on with what interested me, my intellectual development during this period. I wrote a good deal about that. Indeed, I thought I gave rather a fine account of what is, after all, no easy matter to describe. I was quite proud of it after I had finished.

And then what happened? I made the serious mistake of coming downstairs to fetch myself a cup of coffee. (No-one had thought to bring one up, of course.) Constance and Bonnie were sitting side by side at the kitchen table, swirling huge mucky potatoes around in bowls and having one of their little chats. (Ally calls it The Coven — and gets away with it. He has a bit of a way with women.)

Constance greeted me cheerily enough.

"Things going well down Memory Lane?"

I reached for the coffee pot. Some idiot had left it standing with the handle directly over the hotplate and, not thinking to use an oven glove, I burned my fingers. It really hurt. As I made for the sink, the sheets of paper tucked under my arm slithered to the floor, and while I was holding my hand under the cold tap, Constance reached down for them.

"'Chapter Two,'" she read. "'Oxford.'" Then, shuffling nosily: "Any new and exciting disclosures?"

I hadn't much hope of putting her off, but I did try.

"We-ell," I said. "You'll see there's a pretty no-holds-barred account of the First Leamington Conference and ensuing papers. And I don't think I pull any punches about the way I came to the conclusions I did concerning the consequences for compactness in some of the more rarefied infinitary logics."

"Come off it," said Constance, still riffling. "You were an undergraduate. You were *young*." She passed a page at random to Bonnie. "Read out a good bit, Bonbons."

Bonnie, in my opinion, falls in all too promptly with Constance's pantomimes concerning my work. She stood up, quite unnecessarily, to read out in a school-assembly monotone: "'. . . and in my second year at Magdalen I published the first of two papers which were to present a theory of classical and constructive objects. The objects in question belonged to a hierarchy that began with certain basic domains of individuals. The hierarchy then simultaneously extended upwards, in both a classical and constructive direction. Thus it contained classical and constructive functions on the basic individuals, but also classical functions on the constructive objects and constructive functions on the classical objects. The theory did not attempt to provide a constructivist account of the constructive objects. Rather, a topological conception of these objects was presupposed. Thus a constructive function on individuals was regarded as —'" Reaching the bottom of the page, she stopped short, made a thoroughly disdainful face, and sat down.

Constance, meanwhile, shuffled dramatically through the remaining pages.

"Thus a constructive function on individuals was regarded as what?" she demanded, holding one page after another at arm's length to read their first lines. (Pure burlesque, this; Constance's eyesight is better than mine.) " 'An expression that contains no classical types? A topological space? An over-cautious attitude towards the possibility of combining classical and constructive modes of reasoning?' Or this, whatever it is when it's at home with its boots off." She held out yet another page, across the top of which was written, perfectly clearly: "an automorphism on φ".

"Hand it over, please," I said as politely as possible. "I'm going back upstairs now."

Constance reached out for the page she had passed along to Bonnie and slid it, without even bothering to look, upside-down somewhere amongst all the others.

"Well, I wouldn't buy it," she announced. "Not even in paperback. Not till it's been translated into English, anyway."

I prised my precious chapter out of her hand.

"It isn't written for people like you," I said coldly. "It's written for people like me."

"But it's still written for people. And it's the chapter on your youth." She waved the potato peeler about. "Where's all the roller-coaster ups and downs? The adolescent uncertainties? The social and emotional development? Where's Sadie Devereux?"

"I'm not putting her in!" I said, horrified. "I'm still trying to forget her!"

Bonnie, thank God, could get no further than "Who's Sa —?" before Constance interrupted.

"For heaven's sake, Olly. Keep on like this and all you'll manage to write is your very own hagiography. You can't just leave huge chunks of your life *out*."

"Believe me, Constance," I told her, "I haven't taken a whole summer off important philosophical work simply in order to satisfy the prurience of ghouls like yourself about my sexual failures and embarrassments. This autobiography has a serious intellectual purpose. It's aimed at serious readers — scholars in similar fields to my own, for example. People who take an interest in the ideas I've had, and want to know how it was that I came to develop them. Basically, I'm writing for people who want to know about my intellectual life, not my sex life."

"The size of your head," said Bonnie. "Not the size of your pr —"

"Bonnie!"

I'll tell you what's wrong with my elder daughter. She's spent far too much time alone with her mother. She buys her mother's line on everything — especially on me. But Constance is at least kind at heart, even after everything. After all, she has shared my life. She watched me try (and fail) to turn into that other species entirely, the married man. She watched me suffer just as much as herself from my total inability to become the sort of fellow she needed, the sort of husband and father I'm not, and never will be. (Ally, in short.) Bonnie, though, won't even try and understand. She marries the knee-jerk responses of rabid feminism with the horrible jackboot mentality of youth. She judges me far too harshly. Sometimes she doesn't even like me. I don't blame Constance for the sad fact that things with Bonnie ended up this way. (I have no trouble with Nance.) Constance needed a confidante, and Bonnie was a sweet child: sensitive, loving, protective — and always there. Poor Constance wasn't to know that each time she ended up sitting in the kitty litter snivelling her heart out after one of our tremendous rows, or banging the door in my face as if I were dangerous, or shrieking her devastating insults at my departing back, another frozen little splinter ran into Bonnie's soft heart. Constance and I are fine now. Towards the end we'd faced up to one another so often over the marital barricades, we had a really good line in damage limitation and ready truce. Bonnie's the casualty. Like one of those children in war-torn places, she watched far too many small atrocities too young from behind mother's skirt. The last big battle was three years ago, but all the ice in Bonnie's heart still hasn't melted. She still goes round with pockets filled with stones.

"That wasn't very funny, Bonnie."

"Sorry."

"I should think so. Besides, this conversation is between me and your mother."

More's the pity. Constance is flailing the peeler about again.

"So you're not putting in anything at all about that poor girl you trailed round Oxford for weeks and weeks on end?"

"Amy Vanderpole? No, I certainly am not!"

"Or that posh girl you shared a bed with after a party, and lay awake all night, not daring to touch?"

"No, Constance. I'm not putting her in, either."

"Well, what about that fat girl on the cheese counter at Woolies who saved you the large bag of assorted droppings? Are you going to tell about the time you threw up on her sandals at the St Giles Fair after that ride on the revolving teacups?"

"Of course not. Don't be so silly, Constance."

"And nothing *at all* about that evening with Sadie Devereux?"

"No! No, no, no! That bloody evening was, without a doubt, the most humiliating experience of my whole life!"

"That's not what you've always said before."

"Really?" (I'll say one thing. Living with Constance is a continual education.)

"No. You've always said before that the most humiliating experience of your whole life was when you were undergraduate chairman of the Mathematics Colloquium and had to take Professor MacFie out to Giovanni's for dinner. You said you asked the waiter to bring two bottles of wine, and nearly fetched up in tears when Professor MacFie corrected you in front of everyone: "Not Chee-anti. *Kee*-anti.""

"I expect that, over the years, I've developed a sense of proportion about such trivia."

"You mean you've forgotten?"

"Yes, Constance. That's exactly what I mean."

"Well, what about the time you went for an interview for that job at Sussex?"

"What about it?"

"You said that was pretty humiliating. You said the fleas in your trench coat started hopping about just as you were explaining the central theory behind your research, and Dr Marjorison asked you if you'd mind dropping your coat outside the door, so she and the rest of the committee could give their full attention to what you were saying. Have you forgotten that, too?"

Do you suppose that Bertrand Russell had to put up with this?

"Please, Constance. Must we?"

Constance turns back to her bare-arsed potatoes.

"Suit yourself, Olly. It's your book, after all. If you want nothing but a complacent little academic

32

whitewash job, go right ahead. I'll tell you one thing, though. None of that Leamington Conference and ensuing papers garbage is going to get this autobiography anywhere near the bestseller lists. What happened between you and Sadie Devereux might shoot it up to the top."

"Dad. What did happ—?"

"Constance, try and take one simple fact firmly on board. I'm not a pop star. I'm a philosopher. People aren't interested in what I did with Sadie Devereux. They're interested in the way I work."

"What *did* you do with Sa—?"

"Bonnie! Stay out of this!" (Are everyone else's children this bloody nosy?)

"The way you work . . ." Constance is thoughtfully stabbing a potato's eyes out. "Now that might be worth reading about." Her face lights up. "I could write that bit for you. I know how you work."

"No, thank you," I told her firmly. "I'll do it myself."

I'm safe up here again now, but still she's upset me. I'm flicking back through what I've written, and I'm no longer quite so sure I did a thorough job. Constance is right. Where are the uncertainties, the ups and downs? Where's the emotional development? There must have been some. Take that awful business of my following Amy Vanderpole everywhere, week after week, even though she'd made it perfectly plain that she didn't want me. (I must say, she must have been frightfully patient. I wouldn't have stood for it. If some woman started trailing me about against my will, I'd give her one warning then turn round and biff her.) What can have driven me to persecute poor Amy Vanderpole in that extraordinary way? A bit of the old Rosen genetic inheritance leaking through under the stress of a new life? Or was I head over heels in love? If I was, it's left absolutely no trace. Maybe I simply fancied her a bit, and had no idea of how to behave. I can't, after all, have known much about women: no sisters, no girls at school, no female relations unless you count Granny Ruth, and I certainly didn't. It still seems odd, though. Let's face it, Ally has no sisters either, and he even went to one of those ghastly Scottish schools. But I can't see Ally stubbornly flat-footing down the street behind the love of his life — not after she'd turned round and shooed him off once or twice, anyway. I think, quite honestly, I must have been a little cracked.

I did have odd moods, I remember that. Take, for example, that very first train ride. I kept the suitcase and all my carrier bags clamped firmly between my knees, not realizing that luggage had its own place till that old man leaned forward, touched my arm, and raised his eyes to indicate the purpose of all that netting above me. After I'd obediently heaved everything up there, I was at least more comfortable. And I had one of the seats by the window. Leaning my forehead against the cool glass, I watched the countryside between my home and Oxford spinning past — quite literally spinning, I realized for the first time. What's closest rushes back the way you've come, the centre holds, and everything far off moves in its stately way towards where you're going. It's an elementary enough observation. There can be scarcely a traveller on the planet who's failed to notice it (apart from Constance, of course, who was astonished when I pointed it out). But that day, for some reason, it triggered feeling. I sat staring, I've no doubt perfectly blankly, out of the window. But, inside, pleasure grew and mingled with relief. Had I done it? Had I really got out? Had I, like Finn and Gerry and Sol, got away? Who could doubt it? There was my suitcase, up above my head. This was me. Here in my pocket was my ticket, designated "single". The man at the barrier glancing at tickets had failed to bat an eyelid as I walked past. People left home all the time, after all. Fields flashed by. Sun sailed out, mocking my last doubts. Confusion gave way to exhilaration. No-one could get me now. I'd got away! My fingertips tingled. My feet went heavy in my new brown shoes. I suddenly felt alive all over. It was as if I could sense air in my lungs and blood in my veins. I could hear all the whirrings and thumpings and beatings inside me. I'd got away. I had escaped!

Everyone in the carriage was staring. For a moment I couldn't for the life of me think why. (No-one at home had ever bothered to warn me I'd fallen into the habit of thinking aloud.) But even when I realized why they were eyeing me so strangely, I didn't care. I saw that nothing mattered now, unless I chose to let it. I was *free*.

Is that why the very first thing I did when I arrived was to throw up my music scholarship, and switch to philosophy? Did my whole life get changed that day simply because, out of the ambit of my father's cavilling control at last, I wanted to prove I could exercise my freedom? Do I regret it? Would I do it again?

Hard question. Not sure. I know this much: for years and years I secretly held to the view that I had done nothing too drastic that day. I was still Revilo Nesor, King of Mars. I would, in time, write great philosophy and compose great music. What my galactic inexperience didn't allow for, of course, was the black hole of that unassuming little expression "in time". For Time is what it takes. Great music doesn't write itself. Neither does great philosophy. How old am I now? Forty? It doesn't bear thinking about. It's appalling. My life's half over and yet, if you asked me, I'd have to say I honestly feel I've barely had time to get started. I could live for a thousand years, and still want more. There's never enough Time. I could have been a composer, of course I could. There are whole trunks stuffed full of my immature compositions along at the other end of the attic (Constance was nagging on about them only last night, insisting that Bonnie will need at least two of the trunks when she goes off to college). What's in them is mostly only trite and brief efforts, but they raise good ghosts. I only have to pull out one of those dingy old manuscript pads and play through a few pieces to be overwhelmed with freshly disinterred resentment against all those spoiled contemporaries of mine, with their fine instruments and regular lessons. But I'm the one who won the music scholarship. They might have had more of a head start. I had more talent.

But not more time. Back then, of course, I hadn't realized. Like everyone else that age, I was still immortal. The Grim Reaper hadn't yet moved up behind, causing me to glance so uneasily at clocks and calendars as I pass them. In fact I thought that I could not only do great philosophy and compose great music, but also, astonishingly, waste time! I must have spent hours spreadeagled under the belly of that vast college Bechstein, sulking, during the hours playing was not permitted.

I've gone whole weeks without a piano since. Not here, of course. My wonderful Rönisch is here, in the living room. Constance still has it "because of the children". (I'll tell you what that amounts to: twenty minutes of Bonnie showing off to a friend last week, and one whole bloody afternoon of Nance and that stringbean from next door thumping out "Chopsticks" the day that it wouldn't stop raining.) Anyway, it's been exhilarating to play it again — not just because it gets on Ally's nerves, but also because it's such a powerful instrument. It sings at you. It thunders. It roars. I can't quite make the sound I could before Constance put in the carpet and hung up those curtains. But I can have a bloody good try . . .

And sometimes feelings come back. I can root through all the old music which Constance has shovelled into a cupboard (and keeps begging me not to forget when I leave), and sometimes I'll find something I'd completely forgotten. A sonata. A study. I won't think anything of it when I pull it out from its toppling pile, make sure it's got all its pages, and check that Nance hasn't coloured in so many of the notes it can't be read. But when I sit down to play, something odd happens. I won't hear myself. I'll hear only what I heard the first time — the performance that drove me out to buy the music in the first place. And it's not just Rubinstein or Gilels or Barenboim who comes alive again. (Excuse me, Barenboim, but you know what I mean.) It's how I felt — all the original force and power of the mood. Almost impossible to believe that, if I once had feelings half as strong as these, they can have been absent for half an hour, let alone twenty years.

Mind you, some of them haven't. Some of my feelings have been pretty dependable bedfellows, then till now. Which? Well, unhappiness, of course. Solitude. Frustration. Though I am prone to fluctuations of mood, I have to admit that the prevailing streak is one of gloom. I'm not a happy man. I have my moments, just like anybody else. I'm capable of tossing off the shroud at parties, for example. I enjoy parties. I rarely drink in the week because it interferes with my thinking, so when I down tools properly at the weekend and have a couple of glasses, a whole other side of me comes to the fore, and anyone meeting me for the first time would get a very different impression of what I'm like. Please don't misunderstand. I'm not one of those workaday miseries. I've always been affable enough with my colleagues. I wouldn't cast a pall over your lunch. I don't weep in my teacup. But I'm not *happy*.

Take Ally, out there in the garden with Nance. She's squealing with pleasure, and every now and again I hear him chuckling. Lord knows what they're doing. Maybe he's threatening to attack her with his spade each time she puts a foot near one of his tenderly nurtured flower beds. (I paid for all that tender nurturing, by the way. He was our gardener before he went up in the world and became my successor.) Maybe she's heaving lumps of compost at his head. Maybe he's using his dobber, or dabber, or whatever it's called, to plant her precious popcorn. I don't know. But whatever's going on out there, they certainly sound happy. You'd expect that from Nance — she's just a child. But Ally could have told her to shove off hours ago (she seems to have been squealing for ever). I think he must be happy too.

Well, I'm not like that, and I never have been. I moped round Oxford in a favourite old mac (which, of course, Constance threw in the bin along with most of the rest of my wardrobe shortly after we met). I composed soulful music that filled me with even stronger feelings of self-pity than come quite naturally to one of my temperament. I can't think what I was so miserable about. I've always put it down to women (or lack of them) but, looking back, I don't see really how it can have been that simple since, apart from accompanying a couple of wind instrumentalists from the Girls' Grammar through their grade eight, I'd never had any contact with women anyway. And I can't have been broke. I had more money than I'd ever seen. I certainly didn't miss anything from home — unless you count the cat. I had considered bringing that with me, worried it would go hungry during my absence. No-one else ever seemed to notice it prowling, famished, round the house. And when they did their attitude wasn't encouraging. Once, two months into a gross of tuna-flavoured catfood tins my father had bought fire-damaged in a warehouse sale, I came home with an unscorched tin of rabbit chunks, to make a change. "Don't," he warned me sourly. "You'll only spoil it." But in the end I even left the cat behind. I wasn't sure about the college rules (I lost the handbook on the day it came), and the only cage in which I could have taken it was the one Gerry constructed out of rusty old bits of meccano to carry it to the vet that time it went septic.

Apart from the cat, though. How about the card games we played for hours and hours and hours? Did I miss them?

Not really, no. I mean, unlike most things about that house, I didn't mind the card games. We were good players. You could get a good game. I can beat anyone at anything now. I have a really hard time not beating the children. Constance goes all snitty on me: "Winning is not the sole point of the game, Oliver!" But I can't help it. I'd rather give myself a handicap so stringent I'm almost bound to lose — half the cards, only one of my turns in every four — and still play my hardest. And the children are getting better. They do win sometimes (though you would never think it, to hear Constance grinding on and on at me each time I happen to win a round of Snap). Some things change down the years. The children don't mind losing any more. But Constance still minds me winning, so some things don't.

I'd like to think I've changed: left that lank-haired and sullen genius where he belonged, sulking under the Magdalen piano, and —

What's this? What the hell's this? What a cheek! Look what she's had the nerve to get one of the children to slide under the door: her latest contribution to my

40

autobiographical researches, scrawled on the back of the Parish Magazine. I thought at first that that scrabbling was just Nance, or Ned, or that stringbean from next door involving my attic door in one of their verminous games. But look here, opposite the vicar's suggestions for altar flower rota during that difficult holiday period — Constance's own, inimitable handwriting:

The Way He Works

Well, of course, for one thing he slouches. He slouches worse than anyone I've ever seen, and don't forget we've got a teenager. Everyone's remarked on the way that he ruins his jackets, even if they are only cheap green corduroy ones from C & A. Mostly he lies on his stomach on the floor, with his papers spread round him like an untidy fan branching out under all the large pieces of furniture where they get lost, causing him to panic and rush about the house making nasty and unfair accusations. When he gets stiff, he moves up to the desk and spreads the pieces of paper he's actually writing on in a thin layer over the silage of yesterday's working. Gradually, as he gets into it, he forgets there's more layers underneath, and starts stirring everything up with his elbows.

A lot of the time he leans over the desk making great barriers with his arms, as if he's expecting people to sneak in and copy his lemmas and proofs and whatevers. We used to get told off for sitting like that at the table, "Stop it," my father used to say. "No need to fence your food in. It is dead."

Sometimes Oliver lays his head down upon his papers as if they were a snowy breast, and moans and mutters to himself in bursts. He clutches his hair and glowers. He gets up and paces round the house, not seeing anyone and shouting "What?" at you if you make the mistake of speaking. I'm used to it, of course. So are the children. But other people find it really nerve-racking. He's frightened next door's Avon lady several times when she's popped in to leave their soaps-on-ropes, and a passer-by once glanced through our windows, and then telephoned St Crispin's without even asking.

He also writes himself notes, all over his rough work. The page fills up with his endless φs and $d(\xi A)$s and $\forall f,g(f:A \cong B \ \& \ g: B \le C \to f.g: A \le C)$s, or whatever it is that he's working on. And then the notes start appearing at all angles all over the page. "This may yet work," he'll write to himself in the margin, or "The problem, then, is with an infinite anti-chain." Swooping down from the top, he'll have scribbled: "The whole thing really hinges on incomparables." And down in the left-hand corner, printed very neatly, may be a little "Ah-ha!"

It was this kind of thing that made me wonder, when I first met him, if he were off his trolley. This strange little Chinese friend of his called Tinny, or Tunny or something, assured me he had a remarkable mind. But men are always going on like that, insisting one another are geniuses, or fools, as if they can't face the fact that most of them are just mediocre. I didn't rate Tenny's opinion too highly. He couldn't even speak very good English.

But my mother, too, had enormous confidence in Oliver right from the start. "He got ten O levels, didn't he? And four As. I think you'll find men are a bit like Hoovers, dear. If they pick up a lot at the start, then they'll go on picking up for ever."

I still had doubts, though. Oliver seemed so *odd*. He had such difficulty with the simplest things. It was painful to watch him struggling to tie an apron bow behind his back (he uses a peg now), and he'd have to glower at a clock face for several seconds before coming up with a confident reading. I took time to come round to everyone else's way of thinking about him, I have to admit. If I'm honest, it was only after he started winning all those fellowships, and being invited all over, and publishing reams of stuff that I gave up wondering. They couldn't all be wrong, I thought.

And now it seems they weren't. Because even by Oliver's own rather tough standards, he's had a pretty good time of it so far. I can remember a morning when, in one post, he had a letter asking him to give the Presidential Address at the annual meeting of the Royal Philosophical Association, a feeler from a swish American university about their new Chair of Mathematical Philosophy (the same swish place he has a job now — if you can call something that's all pay and no duties an actual job), and a copy of one of the reviews of his first book, in which some big cheese in his field described his work as "seminal", "a landmark in twentieth-century philosophical thought comparable in importance to Russell and Whitehead's *Principia Mathematica*", and "a work of outstanding intellectual maturity, especially in view of the author's youth".

Of course it wasn't actually Oliver's brains that attracted me. It was his body. Well, not even his body really, though I admit I like that well enough. It's sort of solid and cuddly, even if he does have the coldest feet I've ever come across. Meeting Oliver's feet by accident under the bedclothes in the middle of the night is like laying your toasty warm toes against slabs of fish fillet. You wake up panicked every time. I think that might be why I now sleep the way I do, curled safely in a ball, facing the wall.

But that's just feet. Feet aren't important. What's wonderful about Oliver is his face. It's so powerful and grumpy. I don't suppose he'll bother with a photograph on the book jacket. Pity. Academics are such snobs about that sort of thing. But if he did, and if he chose any one of the hundreds of photographs I've taken of him over the years, I can tell you right now what it would look like because they all look exactly the same. He's got this expression of reined-in annoyance on his face (. . . *last* thing I want is to stop and have a photo taken but, on the other hand, don't want to appear to be uncooperative . . . marriage a matter of give and take, after all . . . just hope the whole silly business doesn't take too long and I'm not expected to chat and lose my train of thought . . .). I think these photos of poor Oliver sum up the essential quandary of his daily life. Cover the top half and you have a mouth that's halfway to trying to be smiling and companionable. Cover the bottom half and the eyes have it: that massive brain power held in check yet again for yet another stupid bloody interruption! But he's a striking-looking fellow, with his

44

unkempt hair and lovely brown eyes and beautiful, beautiful mouth. "Gissakiss Olly" my flatmate used to call him, and just the sight of him beetling around a corner muttering to himself used to drive me crazy. (Still does, of course — but not quite in the same way.)

Mind you, I wasn't bad-looking either. I, too, had my admirers. It's not one of those cases of "What on earth made him marry her?" More, "How come neither of them had been snapped up before?"

Well, his hair would have put off a lot of people. It takes true vision to see through the quart of Silvikrin for Greasy it took, and that long afternoon with the rusty nail-clippers. I think I must have second sight. From the moment I saw Oliver Rosen, my fingers itched to pick up a sharp pair of scissors. (Still do, of course — but once again, alas, not quite in the same way . . .)

The fact is, I fancied Oliver from the start. There he was sitting alone in the corner of the pub, staring morosely into his beer and — ping! — I was interested enough to wander across and spill my drink on him. (Well, why else would he bother to wear a mackintosh indoors?) When, half an hour into the conversation, he came up with the fact that his favourite song was "Take my Hand, I'm a Stranger in Paradise", I was a goner.

We went to bed together the very first night. Well, not exactly bed. He offered to chum me home, and we set off down that shadowy shortcut beside the brewery car park and —

Yes. Well. I think I ought to knock off and phone Ally's old Ratbag now, to check Ned can't possibly be spared, not even for one measly hour, to come swimming with his own father and me and Nancy. You can go on from here, can't you, Oliver, now that I've started you off?

Oh, ho, ho, ho. See? Not quite as easy as you thought, is it, Constance? Full, frank disclosures slip off the end of the pen easily enough when you're going on about my funny habits and greasy hair. But I notice the moment we start sailing close to Great Confessions That Might Upset Your Mother you can't clam up bloody fast enough. Well, what about upsetting me? I suppose that doesn't matter. I'm very conveniently expected to be so lofty-minded, so lounged up to the eyeballs with abstract thought, so rolled up in the intellect, that I don't mind the world and his wife knowing that I used to get dandruff.

Well it wasn't my favourite song, Constance. I didn't even realize it had bloody words. As I remember, I merely hummed the tune. It was you who sang. It was one of my favourite melodies, that's all. Borodin. Polovtsian Dance from *Prince Igor*.

"Borodin?"

"That's right. Alexander Porfir'yevich Borodin, 1833-87."

She's stopped wringing out the swimsuits. She's looking quite astonishingly upset.

"Not just —?"

"I'm afraid not."

"And you'd never even heard the words before I sang them in the pub that night?"

"Never. And, if you must know, I thought they were sentimental and embarrassing — a slick denigration of a lovely melody. If I'd known you even a little bit better that night, I'd probably have asked you to keep your voice down."

The soggy swimsuits get me right between the eyes.

"Want to know what you are, Oliver? You're a real turd! If we were still bloody married, I'd bloody kill you!"

I'm halfway to the door before I see Ally's standing there, silently watching. Usually if he and I come together in a passage or a doorway, it's Ally who steps back. This time he holds his ground and, as I go past, the look on his face is really quite unfriendly.

My shirt front's sodden wet, but it was worth it.

CHAPTER
THREE

I found a dry shirt in the airing cupboard. It was too big for me, it must have been Ally's, but it was comfortable. I was just buttoning up the sleeves when, up the flue, I heard the two of them nuzzling downstairs. "Oh, Ally!" "Oh, Constance!" He must have pulled her over towards him, beside the boiler. "He's *awful,* isn't he?" "More bloody trouble than Ratbag!" "It's getting to be like Christmas all over again." "Oh, Constance!" "Oh, Ally!"

It swept me right back. I used to work in here, in this tiny little laundry-room, before the central heating was put in, and Constance insisted I move up to the attic. I must have spent hours heaping up sheets and pillowcases and mattress covers in different ways against the pipes running up the back of the cupboard, trying to blot out the sound of their voices down in the kitchen beneath, going on about me. It wasn't the involuntary eavesdropping I minded. It was the distraction. It used to drive me mad. I couldn't work. It's bad enough having babies and small children. I didn't need all the hours they didn't manage to chew up ruined by hearing Ally's shocked tones rumbling up the pipes:

"You've never been left to cope with all this lot!"

That was his line from the start. I can recall the very

first time I swung the airing cupboard door open in search of a few towels to pad the rickety wooden chair I used to sit on, and caught, quite unmistakably, the sound of the back door scraping over floor tiles, and Ally calling.

"Mrs Rosen. Mrs Rosen!"

After his money, no doubt. He used to spend so much time doing our garden, I probably paid his mortgage as well as ours. I hope Ratbag's grateful. Ally has certainly never leaned over backwards to show his appreciation, unless you can interpret wife-stealing as a thoughtful and imaginative expression of thanks.

"Mrs Rosen! Are you in there?"

Even I began to wonder. I could hear, up the pipes, the sound of Bonnie banging wooden spoons on saucepan lids, or whatever it is children of that age do to reduce everyone round them to whey-faced, snarling wrecks. Nance was quite quiet, so she can't have been born yet. No, that's right. Constance was pregnant.

"Are you all right?"

She wasn't, as it happened. Well, there was nothing actually wrong with her. It was just that she was sitting out of sight behind the table in a huge puddle of three smashed milk bottles, snivelling. That's where he found her.

"You're crying," he accused her. "Over spilt milk." And then he added wisely: "There's no use."

I didn't hear her laugh. She must have just smiled. I only heard years later in one of our Marriage Guidance sessions that she'd been sitting in that pool of milk and broken glass, trying to pick out the best-shaped sliver to make a proper job of slashing her wrists. I ought to be grateful to Alasdair Huggett. I ought to bless the day he pushed open our back door and knelt beside my wife and made her smile, saving my precious Nancy's life. In fact, I deeply resent him — fucking Sir Lancelot. Don't misunderstand me. I don't for a moment mean I wish any harm at all had come to Constance. Of course not. What I mean is, from the moment he lifted her to her feet and slid the milk-sodden smock sprinkled with glass safely off over her head, and carried her from the room, crunching his great gardening boots over the mess he later cleared up so beautifully (and milk's the *worst* — I've heard my mother-in-law say so several times, seeking to justify her daughter's breathtaking variation in domestic arrangements) answer me this: what chance did I have? None at all.

The fact is, I'm not by nature a good family man. It isn't in me. I'm just not that interested, the same way I'm not that interested in soccer, or modern art, or left-wing politics. I see there's something in them all. I even hold views. But that's the limit of it. I don't — and can't — take the same living interest Constance does in the minutiae of family life. Take children's minds. I recognize they're odd, I do see that. I know that babies can be reduced to paroxysms of mirth by being held up to fiddle with the light switches. I know toddlers take quite complicated precautions against being sucked up the nozzle of the vacuum cleaner. I know no small child will even open its new colouring book till it's felt-penned its fingernails ten different virulent shades, and that the stuffed animal of the moment has to be offered some pudding, and if you even suggest to a plainly exhausted child that it goes off to bed it will give you a look of such potent malevolence that you'll wonder why you ever thought it was tired in the first place. I *know* all that. I just can't take an interest like Constance can. I can't answer questions like "Where did Nance learn how to tuck her thumbs in the belt of her jeans like that?" and "Oh, Olly! Isn't her hair just like sunshine?" I simply don't know what to say.

Not that Constance spent the whole of their early years admiring their pert cowboy stances and sunlit curls. Prom the day she brought Bonnie home from the hospital, the cornerstone of Constance's philosophy of child-rearing appeared to me to be: if I spend enough time worrying, they *might* be safe . . . With the result that now, after nearly fourteen years of resolute anxiety, she sees the whole world differently from other people. She has a lot of visions. You have to bear with her. Where you or I see a clean-flowing river and a good picnic place, she sees a sudden drowning or, at the very least, bare feet and broken bottles. Where I see a stunning view from the top of the tower, she sees the gap in the railings and the sheer drop. And after that stringbean next door was born and trundled round to be admired in an Edwardian pram that had taken her mother a full six weeks to restore, Constance's response was little short of demented. "You'll have to sell it! It will have to go! Those handles are just the right height to poke a child's eyes out!"

From the first day, keeping the children alive with all their faculties intact absorbed almost all of Constance's time and energy. No-one was safe from her strictures, especially not me. "Don't let her eat that!" "Don't leave the saucepan handle sticking out!" "Don't leave your razor there!" "Don't run the hot in first!" Thank God children grow up. In the end, and more fairly, the causes of all these grinding reminders become the victims. "Don't sit so near the telly!" "Don't kiss the dog!" "Don't climb in abandoned fridges." "Don't go near Alsatians." "Don't felt-pen on your skin." "Don't eat the red Smarties." You only have to spend half an hour listening to Constance to think you've been whisked somewhere worse than the Lebanon.

Not that it ever seemed to bother the children. They let the whole lot float over them as peacefully and unnoticed as clouds overhead. It used to drive me mad. What I couldn't stand was the sheer inconsistency, the randomness of household patterns. It was like living in a buttercup field that had been heavily mined. One day you'd stroll downstairs to find Constance tenderly peeling four wellington boots off the paws of next door's resentful dog. "Aren't the girls clever? Doesn't he look sweet?" The next, you'd have to pull the windows shut against the sound of her shrieks in the garden. "Leave that poor animal alone! How many times do I have to tell you he's not a bloody toy!" One morning she'd glance up from reading the paper to warn mildly enough, "The word from here on scribbling on fridge doors is still *no*, Nance." The next she'd be across the room like a madwoman, slapping and yelling, and terrifying everyone with her bad temper.

"Listen," I'd say. "You can't expect either of them to take the slightest bit of notice of what you say if one day you ignore them entirely when they disobey you, and the next you go totally berserk, screaming like a banshee and listing every single one of their faults from the day they were born. I've told you before what I think. With children, you must be consistent."

She'd grip the edge of the table, her head bowed. "You're quite right, Olly. You did tell me what you thought. And I'd be such a better person if only I listened to you more carefully."

The knuckles whiten. *Up* goes the table. *Off* slides everything.

"Smug pig! Piss off with all your bloody child-rearing advice! Go stuff a lamp-post, Oliver Rosen! Get out of here! Get out! *Get out*!"

So I ask you, whose fault is it that she'd be standing there, dishevelled and desperate, amongst the smashed cups and spillages of yet another hair-raising outbreak of temper? I never asked her to have babies. I asked her not to — not for a few years, anyway. I didn't want them. I'd only just got out of one family prison. I didn't want to start straight away, building another of my own. I told her plainly what I thought. And I was simply not prepared to have the way I felt shrugged off with cheap and shallow psychological interpretations gleaned from her mother's copies of *Woman's Realm*. It wasn't a matter of my not being prepared to grow up and accept responsibility. I wasn't just stubbornly defending my "spoiled male" position as the chief beneficiary of Constance's generous nurturing instincts. (They'd gone off at half-cock anyway. All I seemed to be getting was a ringside view of every wistful glance into a passing pram, interminable bitter complaints about the dangers and drawbacks of every available method of contraception, and daily bulletins on her potential state of fertility.) My objection to starting a family was perfectly adult and perfectly legitimate. I had other things to do with my life. I didn't want to be tied down.

"You are tied down. We're married, Oliver."

"It's not the same."

I was the one who was right. She was wrong. When Bonnie came along it wasn't the same. All Constance's flippant assertions that she'd be "happy to do most of it" were shown up for the nonsense they were within hours of her coming home, stitched up and tearful, from the hospital. It was "Please, Olly, would you just —?" and "Olly, can you —?" and "Olly, I can't quite —" and "Oh, Olly. *Please*." Don't try and tell me the "look" on my face that she kept going on about was that of a grown man put out because he'd been displaced by some wailing six-pound baby. It simply isn't true. The look on my face was the look of a man trying to find a solution to the problem of foundations for category theory, asked for the nth time that morning to find out who's banging on the front door, throw down a nappy, pick up the ringing phone or hold the baby. I sometimes think if I'd had just twenty minutes' peace and quiet for every time Constance interrupted me with one of her please-Olly-it-won't-take-a-moments, I could have proved Fermat's Last Theorem by now.

54

My work takes concentration. It takes time. It isn't a simple matter of thinking along a straight line and stopping anywhere for a short break. The ideas I work on are almost infinitely complex. It's like building towers from packs of playing cards. Each card is part of the idea, and must be held steady in the mind while the whole tower is slowly and precisely constructed. Let just one card slip and the tower falls, and must be built again, almost from scratch. How can you manage that when someone's screeching at you to let the cat in or the coalman out, or find the baby's sucky rag, or pay the milkman? No wonder I ended up barricading myself in the airing cupboard.

Leaving the battleground free for bloody Sir Lancelot. He's wonderful with children. Good job he's a law-abiding citizen. I tell you, if ever the local police need to put together a working profile of Alasdair Huggett they'll have a hard time learning more than one fact about the man up and down this street.

"And what can you tell us about this Mr Huggett?"

"He's wonderful with children."

And other people's wives. He seemed to spend his life leaning against my boiler, keeping my Constance from slitting her throat (or, worse, the children's). And it's not as if he wasn't outspoken in his own quiet way. I've heard him blithely coming out with remarks that would have got me my ears ripped off in a moment. Take the time I came down to fetch a cup of tea, and Constance was standing by the window, rattling her lemon geranium round in its big pot. "Doesn't look very good, does it, Ally?"

"I expect you've been talking to it."

If I'd said that, I would have been a dead man. But she'd take anything from him. The two of them wasted hours chatting about mulching rhubarb and growing blackspot, and all that sort of thing. Though I did have my doubts about whether it was still a purely horticultural friendship the day I glanced out of the window and saw he'd planted CONSTANCE in huge green letters across the bottom of our garden: C for carrots, O for onions, N for nasturtiums, S for spinach . . .

"What's going on between you two?"

"Nothing. I like him, that's all. Do you mind?"

"What do you like about him?"

"Everything. He's a nice fellow. He doesn't glance at the clock when he finds us all still in our nighties at lunchtime. He doesn't scowl when he gets up from a chair and finds squashed pineapple chunks all over his bum. And he notices when the house is clean."

"I go one better than that. I never notice when it's dirty."

She gives me one of her rare smiles.

"It's very sweet of you."

I know it's stupid, but I just can't help it.

"It isn't *sweet* of me, Constance," I tell her. "It's simply the truth. Do you know what your trouble is? Whenever I say something you want to hear, you say how sweet I am, and whenever I say something you don't want to hear, you say how nasty I am. But it's nothing to do with me, that's what you don't understand. It's the truth you're hearing, Constance. The truth. The *truth*."

56

The smile has gone, of course.

"Oh, shut up, Olly! Go away!"

But I did try again, I remember, the very next morning.

"What is it that's so special about this Ally fellow?"

"He talks to me."

"I talk to you."

"No you don't. Not like Ally."

I picked up my coffee cup and walked towards the door, mimicking the slow amiable tones that rumble up the pipes. "I'll tell you what's coming up really nicely this year . . ." She laughed, and came across to slip her arms around me from behind. I turned and gave her a kiss. We could have gone to bed if Bonnie hadn't been cutting up magazines with scissors she might have stabbed herself to death with, and Nance hadn't been patting a lump of plasticine that might have stuck fatally in her gullet. No, no chance of bed. So Constance stayed in the kitchen, fending the Angel of Death off our children for a couple more hours, and I went back upstairs. But I was thinking about it. Constance was right. I didn't talk to her. No, not like Ally. It isn't in my nature. I can't just ramble on about peach-rot, and inner-city riots, and whether the Pope does more harm than good in the Third World. Grow up, as I did, with people waiting to pounce on every single word you say, and you learn not to come out with anything lightly. I still can't, even after all these years. It used to drive poor Constance mad, this inability of mine to keep the hearth warm with the fuel of poorly considered remarks that go to make up everyday chatter. Our marriage was cold ashes in this respect. She never got over hoping, though. And I never learned. "What's your line on this Northern Ireland business then, Olly?" she'd ask, propped up in bed crunching toast and watching the news on the telly. "What do you think?"

There'd be an agonizing silence. I was on trial. I knew it. She knew it. Our entire marriage was on trial.

In the end, and knowing she'd hate me for it, I'd be forced to reply: "I don't know, Constance. I haven't really thought." Looking back now, I can scarcely believe that I didn't find a solution to the problem. All she was after, for God's sake, was simple human company. "You start me off," I should have said to her. "Tell me you think that Britain should withdraw all their troops at once, and I'll give you several arguments in favour of staying. Or, if you prefer, you take a line in favour of even more troops, and I'll argue the opposite. I'll argue anything you like. No problem arguing, Constance. Just please don't ask me what I think. You see, I haven't *thought*."

It never bothered old Ally, not having thought. I heard his half-chewed views on rape, disobedience, voting patterns in the elderly, teenage spending, bottle recycling, late abortion and whether Play-do is truly as non-toxic as it claims on the packet. You name it and I heard Ally's opinion on it come rumbling up our plumbing. And, taking the odd break to listen in, I found out quite a lot about my wife. It turned out she wasn't quite the slightly daring pinko individualist she made herself out to be at Saturday night dinner parties. I thought she came up the pipes as a bit of a fascist.

Indeed, her views on male doctors, old men who buy girly magazines and childless people who keep rottweilers for pets struck me as distinctly illiberal, not to say uncharitable.

Chiming in nicely with her views on me. The trouble with Constance, of course, is that she is a stranger to dispassionate thought. When she chooses, Constance can look at anyone or anything entirely from her own point of view. And you certainly can't depend on Ally to sketch in the other side of the picture. The fellow just trails round worshipping the ground Constance treads on. You'd think lilies sprang up where'er she walked. It is a tribute to the essential malignancy of his former wife's nature that, after being shackled to her, life with Conseance can appear to be nothing but sunshine and roses. I didn't find it such an easy ride, I must say. And I deeply resent all this "Isn't he awful" stuff that keeps floating merrily up the pipework. I am *not* more bloody trouble than Ratbag. And as for things "getting to be like Christmas all over again", what's that supposed to mean? I thoroughly enjoyed Christmas. I thought, considering, the whole thing went off really rather well . . .

Well? Have you been counting them? I have. There's four — four "The Trouble With Constances". He's got a famous nerve, has Oliver Rosen, parking himself in my house — it is my house now — and secretly stuffing my pillowcases with wodges of abuse. I especially resent that bit about seeing things only from my own point of view. *He* can talk. If anyone ever saw the world skew-whiff it was Olly. Look at the things he hasn't even mentioned in The Great Autobiography to which this long (free) visit is supposedly devoted. Our grisly, quarrelsome courtship? Not a word about that. Our drab and horrible wedding? He's left that out, too. (Maybe he's forgotten it — lucky Oliver.) Has he said a word about Solly, except to mention in passing that he's dead? No. No, he hasn't. He's wiped him out, just like he's wiped out little insignificant things like the day that he first became somebody's father. (Get this, folks. When Bonnie was born he thought she was a midget. No, I'm serious. He was convinced she was a midget. It turned out he'd never so much as bothered to glance at a photo of a new born. He simply assumed they were supposed to pop out of the womb looking as large and pink and fresh as those great lumps you see strapped in their prams outside Woolworths, sucking their Milky Ways.)

Mind you, it doesn't surprise me that Olly's blotted out all births and deaths. The poor soul's terrified of both ends of life, hates the mere mention of them, can't bear to reflect for a moment on either. Well, it's no use going round stuffing other people's pillowcases with ancient grouses about the fact that you were occasionally asked to answer a ringing telephone or throw down a clean nappy. No-one can really be happy till they see things straight. So Olly will never be happy on this earth until he comes to terms with two simple facts. One — everything comes to an end one day for everyone, even the King of Mars. And two — some people will still be walking around when he's stone-cold dead and six feet under.

And he's not the only one in his line of work trying to avoid a few unpalatable basics. I reckon most philosophers come out of the very same box. Lovers of wisdom? Pigs can fly! Half the ones I met were pathetic. Pathetic! They could barely tie their own shoelaces. (It's thought quite the thing in philosophical circles, you know, to stroll round not noticing your own woolly unravelling behind you. It's seen as a sign of intelligence. And if you're really gifted, you might end up one of their heroes: unable to get on the right train, or fry an egg.) Frankly, I think the whole lot of them ought to make a vast communal effort to buck up a bit, or consider changing the name of the profession before someone gets them under the Trades Description Act. What's so philosophical about living your life the way they do, unable even to take for granted what is completely obvious to everyone else on the planet? (For *granted*, you understand. It is a *gift*.)

All this "How do I know this chair I'm sitting on really exists?" garbage really annoys me. Oliver got snappy with my mum that day Bonnie was mucking about on the toilet, but, frankly, I was on mum's side. I don't want either of my two growing up like Oliver. You show me a philosopher and I'll show you someone who's stuffed his head so deep in a bag he can barely see daylight. I don't think it's any accident that almost all of them are men. Women have too much born sense to stick at it. Two or three terms is enough, and then, unless they positively want to make the grade in accidentally setting themselves on fire or forgetting where they live now, they tend to shift sideways into something more useful.

No. I've not much time for philosophers. I'm tied up now, of course. But if Ally ever decapitated himself with the hedge clippers, and I were looking round for someone else, I wouldn't marry another to save my life.

Not that I regret being married to Olly. There's no point in regret. These things just happen. I married Oliver when I was twenty, and I think I can honestly say he was my whole world and I loved him madly. By the time Bonnie was born I did still love him, but not madly; and he wasn't my whole world any more either. I never got enough time with him to keep it up because he was always working. I can't say I hadn't been warned, though. I blame myself. It was my own fault entirely. I should have had the sense to call the whole business off the day before the wedding when he got "a nice little idea about intuitionistic analysis" and wanted to work on it before (don't miss this) "wasting a whole week having a holiday".

After we married, things got worse and worse. We spent hardly any time together and, when we did, he always seemed to be thinking about something else. Mind you, he was busy. If he wasn't proving his own proofs, he was proving himself to himself proving other people's. And when he got too worked up to solve problems efficiently, he'd play the piano for a couple of hours to calm himself down. After that he might offer to spend a bit of time with me. But by then I assumed it was only because he'd overdone it, and anyway I was in a great sulk. Besides, I didn't even enjoy it much when he was with me. I always had the feeling he still had some little problem rattling around the back of his mind. Or I suspected he was just using me as a recreational break: time spent with me was time spent gathering strength, as it were, before he hurled himself back into mental strife. I never had the feeling Oliver just wanted to *be* with me. He was always suggesting a walk (clear the head) or making marmalade (doing something useful) or sex (since you're here), and I got fed up with it, and had a baby.

That was my mother's fault, of course. She knew Oliver wasn't keen on the idea because I'd told her. But, "Go ahead," said my mother. "Don't worry. He'll love it when it's born. I know he thinks he doesn't want one now, but after the little poppet's come along, he'll change his mind."

Well thank you, mother. Take a bow. Though I would never dream of saying so to your face, a lot of your advice to me over the years has had its rather severe limitations. But that was the worst by far. By *far*. Because when Oliver said that he didn't want a family, he really meant it. He seems to have omitted to mention in his pillowcase memoirs that I made it equally plain that I *did*. *And* gave him the option of cutting out. But he didn't want that either. He's never satisfied. Well, I'm sorry I didn't realize quite what a terrible pain and frustration it would be for Minor Celestial Royalty to be lumbered with simple earthly fatherhood. But look at the business from my point of view. It isn't very nice to drag through nine months of pregnancy with someone who's making it perfectly clear by his every expression (or lack of it) that he'd prefer the whole affair to turn out to be a terrible mistake, and this fleshy moon his wife is carrying to sink away as stealthily as it arose. Oliver's thoughts were morbid, you could tell. Facing the fact that there was new life in me filled him with terrors of death for himself. When I brought up his tea or his coffee (you'd think, reading Oliver's account of things, he never got either) it was obvious he wasn't handling the idea of the upcoming happy event with any equanimity. He wouldn't look at me, or speak, except to mutter thank you for the tea. He'd keep his head down, staring at the little black logical symbols all over his bits of paper. He looked so anguished and so out of his depth that, to this day, those funny little symbols remind me of swirling and developing foetal cells. You could tell what poor Olly was thinking. If you stretched out a hand to lift his chin, you could read it in his eyes: it will live later than I will; it will be warm in a bed, screwing someone, when I am old and lonely; it will still be alive when I am dead.

Towards the last weeks, he stopped speaking to me. It was horrible. You couldn't, to be fair, call it a sulk. He just became more and more halting and inarticulate. I think my changing body frightened and appalled him, and like someone desperately trying to think of something to say to a deformed stranger, he couldn't find the words. Sometimes I'd catch him watching me out of the corner of his eye, and I knew what he was thinking. I wasn't large and swollen and beautiful. I was horribly bloated. He wouldn't say so — he knew better than that. But I could tell. He started work earlier and finished later, making excuses to stay poring over his papers long after I was safely covered in blankets and fast asleep. Oh, we kept doing it, deep in the dark. But, frankly, I wouldn't have been at all astonished if it had been him, not his father, who thrust that book under my nose, pointing to that mad passage marked with pencil about not having sex in pregnancy in case the poor baby was born half-witted.

I wouldn't put anyone through that twice, especially not me. I just pretended the next baby was Alasdair's. (Not to Oliver, obviously. Just to myself.) I let Ally do all the belly-patting and listening and admiring, and he was very good at it. He was a natural. This was the days before Ratbag, you understand, when Ally was still just a lonesome and timid gardener, longing to graft himself on good root-stock in order to produce fine sports and blooms. And I think poor Ally probably spent at least as much time as I did kidding himself the baby was his. Oh, he tried to play it cool, lifting the mangled old Babygros out of the little suitcase lying, ready packed, in the corner, and asking me: "What are you hoping for this time, Constance? A gnome?" But I knew how much he really cared. And it was no accident he stayed home from the pub every night in the last month and so was on hand to fetch my mother and take me to the hospital and stay with me when it turned out that the trains were absolutely hopeless on Sundays, and Olly couldn't possibly get back in time from the Second Leamington Conference.

And Oliver's wrong. Ally certainly didn't spend his whole life sprawled over our boiler, idly delivering his opinions up the pipework. He was a *real help* (unlike some people not a million miles away from here whom

I won't mention). You didn't even have to ask Ally. He'd stroll in the back door every day round about tea-time, dangling the key of our garden shed from his little finger.

"I'm back round here tomorrow at Fairway's," he'd tell me, lifting a squawking Bonnie out of her high chair, and wiping her eggy fingers on a damp cloth before releasing her. "You don't mind if I leave my tools in your shed?"

"No," I'd say, as he tipped boiling water from the dementedly rattling kettle into the pot and, while the tea was brewing, carried piles of stinking nappies through to the downstairs toilet for a preliminary flush. "No, I don't mind."

"I'll just throw this next lot in the machine for you, shall I?" he'd ask, re-emerging. "Hot wash?"

"Oh, please."

"Don't get up. She'll only stop nursing. I'll bring the tea-tray across."

I don't know how he did it. He was an angel. I felt the same way about Alasdair Huggett as all those wounded soldiers at Scutari felt about Florence Nightingale. As soon as he showed up in the doorway I felt a bit better. He'd only be in the house a few minutes and the curtains were drawn, Bonnie was settled at the table absorbed with her crayons, I had my feet up by a tray of tea, and the rumble of strong machinery efficiently pushing back the frontiers of chaos spread comfortingly through the house. With Ally near me, I could almost cope.

"Stay for a drink?"

"Don't you move. I'll get it."

Where did he come from? Did the fairies send him? And how, I ask you, did he come to me? He'd wipe the table and wash the dishes and tempt Bonnie into her bath, or her pyjamas, or her bed. He'd read *Rumpelstiltskin* every day for a fortnight without ever rushing or skipping or trying to get away with turning over two pages at once. Then he'd kneel down and peel the Play-do off the kitchen floor, and rinse the milk bottles, and check, before the shop shut down the road, that I'd got something for supper. Then he'd companionably settle beside me on the sofa. Sometimes he'd inspect the day's scratches. Sometimes he'd fondle Nancy's little feet. Sometimes he simply sat. He never made a move in my direction (except to point to the little gold safety-pin I was supposed to move from one bra strap to the other to remind me which side to start Nance nursing next time). I put his restraint down to his Scottish schooling, and thought he must have been brought up to think a man's wife belongs to him and you mustn't touch her, the same way you wouldn't dream of switching on his stereo or using his power-drill unless you'd asked him first. Once, only once, when I plucked at the one horrible frock that still fitted and said despairingly, "I tell you, I'm dead fed up with my body," he couldn't help answering promptly, "Well, give it to me, then." But when I turned to offer it, he pretended to be absorbed in *The Autobiography of Bertrand Russell* which Olly had left on the arm of the sofa.

"Do you believe all this stuff, then?"

"All what stuff?"

He stabbed the page.

"All this about Bertrand Russell sitting up in his pram and asking his Aunty Agatha, 'Aunty, do limpets think?'"

"No," I said. "I don't believe that. I think that's rubbish."

"But wasn't Bertrand Russell supposed to be very clever? Wasn't he a great philosopher?"

I shifted Nance before my arm went dead.

"Well, that's what the great philosophers write, isn't it?" I said. "Rubbish." I reached for the book and had a flick through. "Here," I said. "Listen to this." I did my Bertrand Russell imitation, the one that drives Olly clean up the wall. "'I then rode away on my bicycle, and with that my first marriage came to an end.'"

"Is that it? Is that all he says? How long had he been married?"

I skipped back through a goodish chunk.

"Years and years."

"I don't believe it."

"Course you don't. It's rubbish."

"Nobody's marriage ends that easily . . ."

(He looked so wistful I could hardly bear it.)

"Mine may," I said. "If Oliver doesn't start paying me and the children a bit more attention."

Ally looked thoughtfully at the beautiful, button-nosed baby he so much wished belonged to him.

"Strange, these philosophers." He took the book, and riffled backwards through the pages. "'Great god in boots!'" he read aloud. "'The ontological argument is sound!'" But I could tell from the tone of his voice that he wasn't really concentrating.

"They can be passionate," I told him, trying to ease us back on to the topic we both had, oh so shyly, in mind. I prised the book back out of his hands. "Listen. 'We spent the whole day, with the exception of mealtimes, in kissing, with hardly a word spoken from morning till night, except for an interlude during which I read *Epipsychidion* aloud'."

He didn't take the hint. The giant lump just sat there, staring moodily ahead.

"Just like other people in some ways," I persisted. "They have lovers . . ."

"Lovers?"

Could we be getting somewhere? No. Ally was shocked.

"Take Bertie here," I insisted, patting the book. "Terrible bad breath. And yet he had lovers."

I turned a few pages over, and pointed. (I even thought to use the hand without the ring.) "'For external and accidental reasons we did not have full relations that evening, but we agreed to become lovers as soon as possible.'"

Ally was silent.

"Maybe she couldn't find her diaphragm," I suggested, trying to force the conversation up one of those avenues of discussion so firmly barricaded by Scottish school training.

Ally, however, was equally determined to steer it down more wholesome channels.

"I expect that her husband was busy working upstairs."

I was annoyed. I get sick to death of all these bloody men taking such good care of one another's interests.

"Maybe she had cystitis," I taunted him. "Or vaginismus."

Recoiling stiffly, Ally reminded me: "'*External* reasons', he said."

"Labial polyps, then. Or crabs. Or a really bad prolapse."

"That giant hogweed's shooting up again all over the common."

I know when I'm beaten. I gave up. And it didn't seem more than a couple of minutes before Oliver strolled down from the laundry cupboard where, while Ally crashed through the early evening domestic assault course on his behalf, he'd been peacefully proving a lemma, or establishing a theorem, or maybe even deducing a corollary.

"Is there more tea in that pot? Is it stone-cold?"

Ally took himself off. Everything I'd said had made him uneasy, and Oliver's polite but baffled smile finished the job in no time. The minute he'd gone, Oliver glanced at the oven (off), peered in the fridge (almost empty) and looked at me (still sitting comfortably with a drink in my hand). You could tell he was dying to say something about supper but didn't dare, for fear of being snarled at to make it himself.

Instead, he started on another front.

"Is that man after you?"

"No. No, he isn't."

"You sound very sure, considering how much time he spends in this house, chatting about leaf-curl and giant hogweed."

"I am sure. As it happens I just this minute offered myself to him and he as good as said no, thank you, Constance."

"Rude bugger. I'll go after him if you like. Punch his ungrateful lights out."

He's reaching for the teapot, actually. But it's the thought that counts.

"You're a brick, Olly."

His ears prick up. Is it a compliment? He looks round the room again, appraising things a little differently. No supper reaching the peak of perfection inside the oven. Good. No interesting little side-salads on the table that need protecting from the cat. Laundry rumbling away, well in control. One child contentedly in bed, the other comatose in her basket after a restful feed. (All Ally's handiwork, of course. But he's gone home.)

"Well, Constance. If I'm a brick, how about a quick spot of bricklaying?"

"Oh, why not?"

"Come on, then."

"Right you are."

On the third stair I stop, and ask Oliver's departing back:

"Olly, do you really love me?"

It's a moment or two before the bastard even bothers to turn round.

"Of course I love you, Constance."

"You don't *sound* as if you love me."

"Maybe I don't. It's just that I've told you before, that's what gets me."

Do other women get this sort of thing? No wonder they go round with copies of *Perfect Stranger* and *Hold the Dream* stuffed in their shoulderbags.

"Olly, slow down."

"Constance, I'm practically crawling up these stairs as it is!"

"I'm *tired*, Olly. I'm a nursing mother."

"You mean you've changed your mind!"

The tone's already resentful. If I hadn't considered changing my mind then, I'd certainly consider changing it now. While Oliver stands above me, glowering, I wonder what, exactly, I do have in mind. You get so shattered with babies and small children, you get out of touch with your very own brain cells. You have to take time out, clutching the banisters like some poor old dear in the last stages of Alzheimer's disease, desperately trying to clear enough of a pathway to your remaining grey matter to send in a probe. "How does the lady feel, fellas? Brain?" "*Not much going on here, sir. Everything seemed to go a bit numb a few weeks ago.*" "Self-esteem?" "*Can't be located right this minute, sir.*" "Energy level?" "*Dangerously low, sir. Practically rock bottom.*" "Sexual responsiveness?" "*Closed down.*" "Closed down? Then what was all that going on on the sofa with Alasdair Huggett less than ten minutes ago?" "*Can't tell you, sir. But whatever you saw, there was certainly no action on this patch.*" "Well now, fellas. This is a pretty poor lookout. I thought that young doctor at the hospital claimed that this woman was supposed to be healthy! Has no-one around here got anything positive to report? Hormones?" "*On overtime, sir!*"

"Sensitivities?" "*Humming!*" "Nerves?" "*Right on edge!*" "Glands?" "*Working well, sir! See. There's a tear — and another — and another! Look! A whole, glorious deluge of them, sir! She's fit and well!*"

"For God's sake, Constance! What's the matter? What are you crying for? I thought you wanted to come upstairs!"

"Oh, shut up, Olly! What would you ever know about what I want? What do you care?"

Off we go. Curtain up. I know my lines, and he knows his. We're well-rehearsed, so it will be another fine and convincing performance from the young married couple at 23 Bonnington Avenue, a secret like your own. Extraordinary, when you come to think. Half the world knows the rest of this show by heart. I bet they could all shout and weep and grovel and cajole along with us while all the tears end up in sex, and all the sex ends up in tears. And the other half wouldn't believe it if you handed them the transcript and showed them the video. "Oh, no. I'm sure he didn't mean it quite like that!" "Are you sure that's exactly what she said?" "Surely not!" "You can't have heard him properly!" "She called you *what*?"

Do you want to know what I think, Oliver? Oh, no. I suppose you don't. After all, you've just admitted that you spent hours and hours heaping up sheets and pillowcases and mattress covers against the pipes, just so you wouldn't have to listen. It's a pity you hadn't started your memoirs in those days. They would have made really good sound-proofing. That Victoria Plum pillowcase is stuffed practically solid already. You don't mind if I just shovel in this lot for a moment, do you? Better not leave it lying about in case the girls see it, and I'm in a bit of a rush to get back downstairs. I'm pretty sure I can hear Ratbag Row No. 884 just starting up in the kitchen.

CHAPTER
FOUR

I can't believe I've written as much as I have. I had to move on to another pillowcase. There's more hidden away in the airing cupboard than in the pile on my desk now, and I blame Constance. I write so much more easily when I know she won't see it. And she's not proving to be all that helpful either.

"Constance, have you seen my doctoral thesis?"

"Why? Have you lost it?"

"No, I haven't 'lost' it, Constance. It's just I don't know exactly where it is."

"If you can't find it, Olly, then it's lost. That's what all we simple folk have decided the word means."

Of all her irritating lines, this is one of the ones I most dislike: you, Lettered Imbecile; me, Unschooled Clever Kate.

"Constance, could I forego the lecture, and settle for any useful advice that you might care to offer?"

She's really going at that ironing.

"I expect it's somewhere in all that rubbish up there in the attic. You really ought to have a good clear-out, Olly. Suppose you died . . ."

Typical. That's just like her. Ratbag phones up to ruin Ally's morning, so Constance passes the universal thump on to me. "Suppose you died . . ." She knows I can't stand to hear it. She knows it upsets me. It never mattered before. It was just an expression, just words; shorthand for all the sensible small print in my brain about endowment mortgages and wills and insurance policies. I ranked "Suppose you died . . ." along with the tedium of current events on the television: "Suppose the exchange rate worsens, Chancellor?" "Suppose interest rates fall?"

Then Solly died. I saw him drowning, but I never believed he wouldn't show up again later, his old self. I never saw him dead. It was Finn who went up to identify the body when they recovered it a few days later, further along the coast. I went through the funeral pretending I was someone else, I remember. A perfect stranger. Nobody I knew. It felt peculiar, but it seemed to work. The service was senseless, and I kept my eyes right away from the coffin. It was Constance who started the nightmares — oh, not deliberately; but "People aren't clocks," she said irritably months later, when she pulled a paperback out from the shelf and a small chute of sand slid from its spine. "I hate remembering that they've stopped!"

And that very night I began with the nightmares. They weren't dreams. I was not asleep. I lay awake, and couldn't stop thinking about Solly's brain. I couldn't help thinking about all those hours when it was floating in the water, and lying on the beach, and in the morgue. It was entirely unimaginable to me that, during that time, all its force and capacity had been switched off. That was for some reason much harder to accept than the fact that Solly would never come by again in between girlfriends to cadge a bed, or a meal, or some sympathy from Constance. To tell the truth, though I found Sol by far the easiest of my brothers to get along with, still he and I were not that close. I was surprised how sickened and distressed I was by thoughts of his poor brain lying, inert, in its skull. It was a horrible time. Until the nightmares started I'd never understood how people like Constance's mother could bother, in life, to take time out to worry about what was to happen to them after they died. Burial — cremation — what on earth did it matter? But suddenly there I was lying awake night after night for the first time in my life, exhausting myself hurling one little screwed-up ball of rational thought after another against the ghastly image of Solly's still and unwinking brain. I should be grateful that I could, at least, think of it with merciful dispensation from worse imaginings. The tissues must, presumably, have stayed fresh, preserved first by sea salt, then by municipal refrigeration. Good thing he was cremated, I tell you. The way I was haunted, if he'd been buried I'd have had to dig him up to make a bonfire of the soft, furious maggots. "Listen!" I can remember shaking poor Constance awake one black, black night. "If I die — Wake up, Constance! Listen! If I die —"

The bedclothes heaved. The sheer balefulness of her response was, in a funny way, a bit of a comfort.

"*When* you die, Olly . . ."

There are times for compromise.

"If I die *first*, Constance. Promise you'll get me all burned up straight away. No messing. Bribe someone to fiddle the paperwork so I end up at the front of the queue. Do anything it takes, but make sure you get every bit of me burned up at once. Especially my brain."

She was, of course, waking up fast now.

"Give us some of your body now then, on account."

"Constance, I'm serious."

"So am I . . ."

What is it with women? Is it a low boredom threshold?

"Get off. Keep your hands to yourself, please. I'm not in the mood."

"Oh, come on, Olly. You did wake me up."

True.

"Well, only if you promise. Do you promise?"

"I promise, Olly."

"Promise *what*?"

(Just checking. This is important.)

"Get you burned up before you're even cold. Rely on me."

Her hot little hands were winning anyway. You certainly can rely on Constance. And if she promises you an instant funeral pyre, that's what you'll get. She can fix anything. She always could. I didn't even have to worry that, in the morning, she would dismiss as mere nocturnal ramblings what had come out of the dark. All horrors of the night are real to Constance. I've been hauled from the deepest sleeps to hold her shaking body and play the exorcist, then had to listen all through breakfast while she spilled out again, practically word for word, the very same fears about children getting crushed, or lost, or falling on to spikes. There's no relief in mere daylight for the professionally apprehensive.

78

But at least they treat other people's treads with equal respect.

It all sounds so very unhealthy. But when I look back at the years the children were young, truly it seems to me to have been nothing but a long black hole of misery and exhaustion. It can have lasted only for a few short years, but it seemed to go on for ever and ever. The details are mercifully blank now. Press me, and no doubt a few memories would come to the surface. Reminders of bitter frustration. Hostility. Resentment. Despair. I didn't love and care for Constance properly. If I did, how come she worried so, and drank what was self-evidently far too much for her own good, and even, in the worst times, took all the pills those idiots down at the surgery prescribed, destroying utterly what fragile balance she had left? I kept my head down and it didn't help. She needed more than that. But, then again, I had no more to give. She didn't love me properly either. How can you love someone and rail away at them day after day, picking at their blind spots and weaknesses, stripping off their skin? I look at the photographs still hanging on the kitchen wall — me pushing Bonnie's stroller up one end of a see-saw; Constance playing splash pat-a-cake with Nance in a cracked china bowl. And we don't look unhappy. But that's a mystery to me, because we were. Sometimes things were better. Sometimes they were worse. But they were never good. And we're agreed on that, because when in a Marriage Guidance session once the counsellor suddenly asked out of the blue: "But what about all the good times?" I felt for Constance when she turned to me, her eyes pleading for help. I couldn't think of any good times either.

So tell me, what's wrong with us, for heaven's sake? Why are we punished this way? Why can't I live for ever — it's all I want. Why couldn't Constance be happy? She wanted a good marriage more than she wanted an easy life or a pretty face or her share in my index-linked pension. Why wasn't it possible? What went wrong? The only clue I have is that, once, in a restaurant called Chinese Blue Sky, a dish of fortune cookies descended suddenly in front of Constance. All of the children around the table reached out at once, of course. But, smoothly, the waiter swung the dish out of their reach. No doubt about it, he had chosen Constance. Out of the whole group of a dozen people, she was to choose her fortune first.

It was her sheer misgiving that unnerved the rest of us. You'd think she had been asked to choose her life. But when her hand came down, it was quite clear which of the crisp little biscuit envelopes she wanted. We watched her snap it apart, and unfold the message. I know my Constance like I know my own right hand, and if the waiter hadn't still been standing right behind her, she would have read it out in her fake Chinese accent: "You can have what you want most in life. You can't have what you want second and third."

The children puzzled it out. Our older companions simply shrugged and smiled. But Constance, horribly upset, looked straight across at me.

"Oh, Olly! Is that what's wrong?"

Maybe it was. I wouldn't know. I'm not that sort of philosopher, am I? All I can say is, looking round, the theory does appear to fit the facts. Nobody gets it all. Take poor old Ally, he's a case in point. You only had to hear a snatch of his phone call with Ratbag this morning to know that here is a good man being torn apart, paying for one of his heart's desires, in kind, with the other. Even I, scarcely the chief beneficiary of his marital rift, couldn't help giving him a look of sympathy as I inched past. The poor sod was clearly already floundering.

"Don't try to tell me you didn't read the note, Stella! I know you read it. I made sure you did. I stapled it to the cheque!"

Short pause. You could tell from the look on Ally's face that Ratbag was going on and on at the end of the line about how small, or how late, the cheque was.

"Bad blood with money?" I asked Constance amiably, proffering my coffee cup.

She shrugged. "No more than usual."

I glanced at Ally, who was clearly getting trounced.

"I certainly hope she's not able to get her hands on any of the money *I* give you."

Constance quite deliberately upended the coffee dregs into my cup.

"Money is only today's side issue," she announced frostily. "The main theme is dates for the holidays."

"Holidays? Are you lot going on a holiday? You didn't tell me you had any plans."

Suddenly Constance had exactly the same weary look on her face as Ally, at the end of the telephone, had on his. I wasn't going to put up with that. I'd got my coffee, so I left the room.

Nancy was sitting on the stairs, squeezing the cat. All I said to her as I went past was, "I hear you lot are going away on holiday."

She practically went ashen. She stared in horror.

"Holiday? No! Not a holiday! Oh, no!"

Releasing the cat, she charged at the kitchen door and crashed through it. It wasn't like my silent, equable Nance to get in such a state. But I could hear her rounding on Constance, desperately upset.

"Dad says you're taking us away on holiday! You promised me before he came! No holiday, you said! You *promised* me!"

I was touched. Although, Lord knows, I knew the autobiography would go all the better for a bit of sustained peace and quiet, I did think it thoughtless and inconsiderate of Constance to plan on taking the girls away during my summer visit. Out of interest I found myself drifting back into the doorway.

Ally was stretched to the very limit of the telephone wire, trying to carry on listening to the rantings of Ratbag while he prised Nance away from the ironing board. Constance was hastily setting the hissing iron down on the floor.

"Sweetheart! Don't worry —"

"Don't worry!" Nancy was screaming with rage. "Don't worry! That's what you said at Christmas!"

I've never seen poor Nancy in such a frenzy. When Constance reached for her, she broke away. When I reached out for her, she fought me off and rushed from the room. Her howls were echoing through the house as Constance pushed past and took off after her, straight up the stairs. I would have asked Ally what on earth was going on — and to explain all this bloody Christmas stuff they all keep going on about — but he was busy, yelling down the phone.

"Pontypridd? For *five weeks*? That only leaves a miserable week for us! . . . Stella, you know perfectly well what I mean by 'a miserable week' . . . It's thoroughly selfish and inconsiderate of you . . . I'm still his bloody father, you know . . . You'd better, Stella. I'm warning you . . ."

But she'd hung up.

He turned. His eyes were burning in his face like little coals. He wasn't speaking to me. He was muttering to himself.

"I'll kill her. One day, so help me, I will march down my garden and pull up one of my prize-winning leeks and stuff the bugger down her little Welsh throat!"

It's not all that easy to think of something to say to someone who's worked themselves up into such a big tizzy.

"I'd no idea she was called Stella."

Now he was staring at me. He looked unhinged.

"For God's sake, Oliver! What would you ever know about the small potatoes of other people's lives? When have you ever bothered with anyone but yourself?"

Bloody rude. What a fucking nerve! How dare the man stand there and lecture me in my own kitchen! If he weren't bigger than me I would have knocked him down, Great Garden Gorilla. Is it my fault his ex-wife runs rings around him? No, it's not. And I'll tell you something else. I don't care one tiny bit for the way in which he and his lady love, my former wife, have started — oh so subtly for their convenience as matching martyrs — to lump my behaviour together with Ratbag's. I am not like her. She is not like me. So far as I can make out, Ratbag considers no-one but herself as she sails through life, picking the bits of carpet out of her teeth. I, on the other hand, have leaned over backwards trying to meet Constance's expectations and the children's needs. In an ideal world, I would have led a very different life. I think even Constance will admit I did my bloody best. There was a time when she was grateful for my efforts. I tried hard, forcing myself not to snarl when sleep was shattered for the tenth night in a row, disguising my disgust when I got mess from the nappies under my fingernails, or regurgitated boiled egg down my neck. Maybe what Constance says is right, and, left to myself, I might have walked rather gingerly around the two of them, dropping the occasional neighbourly nod, till they grew up. So what? I wasn't left to myself, was I? (Show me the man who is.) And in the end I made it. I learned. I learned to smear cream on to wriggling bums, and wipe up sick, and decide for myself whether whatever it was being stuck up my nose needed winding, or having its head pulled around straight, or hastily wrapping in tissue and flushing away. Is it my fault I was never quite sure of myself with the children? Why should I be? I kept trying. And, prodded by sharp little looks from Constance, I did get better. I learned dutifully to admire small messy works of art, and stick them on the fridge. I attended all manner of ghastly school functions. I ground my way in a responsible fashion through arguments about bikes on main roads, and rises in pocket money, and not keeping rats. Oh, yes. I sodding well earned my laurels. And now, for better or worse, I am their father, and I'm not going to be patronized by Alasdair Huggett. If all I did all day was stroll around snipping the heads off pansies and fretting about the nasty little brown spots on people's leaves, I too could have made a lovely, easygoing husband and father. Not that Stella Ratbag seems to have appreciated his efforts . . .

"I'm not sure I'm inclined to take remarks about my personal failings very seriously from someone who can't even handle his own ex-wife."

"No-one could handle Stella — well, maybe *you* could."

You'd think it was some sort of insult, the way he said this.

"Are you implying I'm insensitive? Well, I'd like to know what good comes from all your sensitivity, Alasdair. People like you are useless when it comes to the crunch."

"That's because we have feelings!"

I wasn't going to take that lying down.

"Your precious feelings don't seem to help you get to see more of your own son!"

He started howling, literally howling. He reeled round the kitchen like a bloody great giant in pain.

"Well, maybe they help my *precious son*!"

I hadn't thought of that. Maybe they did. I must say, before he came out with this anguished bellowing, I'd always thought of Ally as a bit of a fool when, each time

Ratbag reneged on some agreement that didn't quite mesh with her whim of the moment, he rushed out of the kitchen door to gnash his teeth quietly on the back doorstep rather than straight round to her house to tear her apart. But maybe it wasn't weakness after all. Maybe it did help Ned, and Ally really is a Holy Fool.

Not a role I myself would fall into easily . . .

"You ought to send me round. I'd sort her out."

His outburst seemed to have fetched all the stuffing out of him. While he didn't exactly take up my generous offer to go round and savage his wife on the subject of mutually agreeable holiday arrangements, he did at least seem to see it as a sort of olive branch. Sinking on to a chair, he buried his head in his arms. And that's how Constance found him when she came back into the kitchen a few moments later.

"What's the matter with Ally? What on earth have you done to him?"

It's quite extraordinary how offensive Constance can be sometimes, without even trying.

"I haven't done anything to Ally. He's perfectly all right. More to the point, what is the matter with Nancy?"

Constance became evasive. "Oh, nothing. Nothing important. Bit of a misunderstanding, that's all. Nothing to worry about. It's all over. Everything's sorted out now."

I can't say it's common practice for Constance to try to set my mind at rest about anything. I couldn't help instantly becoming suspicious.

"But what was all the fuss about?"

"It wasn't anything, Oliver. It was a mistake. Nancy's fine now. She's perfectly happy. No problem. Let's just forget it."

"Forget what?"

"Oh, Olly. Stop going on about it, *please*. Let it be."

Her colour was high. She looked tense and embarrassed. It was quite clear the last thing in the world she wanted was to explain to me just what it was that had so rattled Nancy. But it's not like Constance to want to keep the lid on anything. It's more her line to go round forcing small cowering secrets best left in the dark precipitately out into searing sunlight. I couldn't work it out. It wasn't right. Something I didn't understand was going on, and, by the looks of it, something no-one was over-anxious to share with me. The two of them made an unnatural little tableau — Ally a broken man, Constance wary but protective by his side. They reminded me more than anything of one of those Victorian paintings: "The Fractured Hearth", perhaps; or "All Happiness Fled". What could have happened to throw everyone in the house so badly? It wasn't like Constance to want to hold her tongue about anything, or Nance to go berserk, or Ally to slump across the table top, the very picture of despair.

Or was it guilt?

I read the newspapers. And though I am a man of immense mental command, and can keep speculation well in control, there swam across my mind a picture of such an appalling nature that it was all that I could do to say calmly and civilly:

"Constance — a word with you in private."

"Oh, Olly. Can't it wait?"

"No, I'm afraid it can't."

She knows my tones of voice, as I know hers. Giving the great hunched shoulders one last pat, she followed me from the room.

I started up the stairs. Constance laid one hand co-operatively on the banister, then failed to get any further.

"Olly, is this important?"

"Yes, it is."

But she seemed desperate to avoid discussion. "It's not a good time. I'm really worried about poor Ally." Her knuckles whitening round the stair-rail, she started up her usual smokescreen: ferocious attack. "Why is he in this state? What on earth was all that howling? I'd certainly like to know what you and Ratbag have done between you, to upset him so badly!"

"And in return," I said, "perhaps you'd be good enough to tell me exactly what the two of you are hiding that has upset my Nancy so badly."

That brought her up a few stairs pretty sharpish. For a moment she looked as if she might be about to burst out with something; but then, with a visible effort of control, she lapsed into an expression both aggressive and shifty.

"I told you, Olly," she hissed. "Nancy is fine."

"If Nancy is fine, why all this secrecy?"

"Secrecy?"

She's like Jane Fonda — simply cannot act.

"Yes, secrecy. You won't give me a straight answer to a straight question. Here we are, standing whispering together on the stairs. What the hell's going on?" I took her arm and pulled her up the last few stairs, and off sideways into the little laundry-room. Bundling her inside, I slammed the door behind us and pinned her up against the airing-cupboard door.

"What's going on?" I asked again. "Why are you acting so shifty? Why is Nance so upset? And why is your precious Alasdair Huggett hiding his head in his hands? What's he looking so bloody guilty about, Constance? Answer me that!"

She'll have bruises tomorrow, on her arms. And I'll have a black eye.

"How dare you? How *dare* you? God damn you to hell, Oliver!" She hurled herself at me like one of the Furies. There are scratches down my face. My shirt got ripped. Even my woolly's got a hole in it.

"I'll kill you, Oliver! I will strangle you! I'll fetch a meat-axe to you! I'll pulp your brain!"

I'm strong enough; and still I only just managed to hold her a little bit away from me, till Ally rushed up the stairs to the rescue. It was a close thing. If he hadn't charged through the doorway and peeled her off, she might have throttled me. I was already going blue.

"What the hell's going on between you two now?"

He looked almost as angry as she did, and she was gurgling with rage.

"This shitbag here reckons that you and Nance —"

Words failing her, she attacked me again. Ally had to pinion her arms, to keep her off me.

"Me and Nance — yes?"

He waited, uncomprehending.

"That's it!" screeched Constance. "Nance and you!"

"Nance and me?"

He was still waiting, his glorious innocence acting the stiff brake on his lumbering brain.

"For God's sake, Ally! The bloody papers are full of it. You must know what the bastard's on about!"

I think light dawned at last. At least, he turned to me, his eyes clouding over with disgust and outrage. Slowly he clenched his massive fist, and pulled it back.

Quick thinking isn't my strong point. I'm more slow and thorough, on the whole. But even I have my moments.

"Constance! How can you? I said no such thing!"

The fist held steady in the air. Ally was waiting for more. Give him his due, he's not the man to go round delivering knuckle sandwiches wrongly.

I must say, terror does lend eloquence.

"The thing is, Ally, I just wanted a quiet word with Constance. That's all. Quite justifiable, in my opinion. As far as I can make out, Nancy has just gone frantic at the mere mention of going away for a few days' holiday. I've every right as her father to ask Constance why. But there's certainly no place for all these lurid assumptions. It just occurred to me that maybe Nancy wasn't getting on too well with you right now for some silly little reason. Perfectly natural. Or maybe she was a bit sick of sharing her mother. I certainly thought it best to ask."

The fist is lowered.

"And that's all you meant?"

"That's what I *said*. I thought I made myself perfectly plain."

You can always depend on Constance to fling a peace pipe straight back in the mud.

"'Guilty', you said. You said that Alasdair looked 'guilty'."

"Only said 'looked'. Never said 'was'."

Looking back, I think this was my big mistake. I suspect that if, rather than slugging her between the eyes with this rather academic distinction, I'd simply accepted the role of repentant worm, she might have let me off the hook. As I have said before, Constance is kind. But I went one step too far, and Constance flew straight into another of her tempers.

"Want to know, do you, Oliver? Want to know *why* Nance is so bloody anxious not to go away? Then I'll tell you! After all, as you so sanctimoniously point out, you are her father and you have a right to know. Last Christmas —"

Ally's huge hand slid over her mouth, rendering her mute.

"Excuse me," I said. "But I would very much like to hear whatever it is my former wife has to say."

Still gripping Constance tightly, Ally lowered his face to mine.

"Listen," he said. "Take it from me, Oliver. Nancy is fine. And there's no plan to take either of them away. There never was. What we were talking about was Ned's school holidays."

"And what's all this stuff about last Christmas?"

Constance squirmed frantically. Ally tightened his grip.

"Nothing," he said firmly. "Last Christmas was last Christmas. And now Constance and I are going downstairs for a few quiet moments on our own before supper."

He bundled Constance out of the door in much the same way I had bundled her in. Pax Alasdair. Good job he's big enough to make it stick. We needed a truce, if only for the sake of the children. The afternoon must have been quite upsetting for Nancy. I'd seen her out of the window, wandering around the back garden in a daze, clutching her precious cat and whispering in its ears, making them twitch.

I've played my part — stayed up here in the laundry room passing the time while everyone downstairs calms down a bit. But I am getting a little hungry now. It's after seven. Taking a cue from the strange smells floating up at the back of the airing cupboard I thought at first that Constance might be out to poison me. I certainly wouldn't put it past her. But then I worked out from a few ill-tempered remarks that rose up the pipes that she was just trying one noxious household chemical after another to lighten the scorchmark on her brand new floor tiles. I shan't say anything when I come down. I don't want to let on I have, in fact, overheard perfectly clearly all the ungenerous things she's been saying about me. But, frankly, I don't see how it was my fault at all. Surely before she followed me out of the room, she should have had the sense to unplug the iron.

Where is my ticket? Where have I put it? It's not upstairs, on my desk, or in my jacket pocket. I bet Constance has taken it upon herself to tidy it away safely somewhere. How am I going to find out where it is and get it back long enough to look at the small print and see if it's possible to shift my return flight forward a week or so? I can't stand much more of this visit. I'm going mad.

The fact is, I have no talent at all for family life. How long was I down there? Little more than an hour. It can't be later than nine now, and here I am again, stuck in this bloody cupboard, really quite upset, wondering what went wrong. Everything started pleasantly enough, for heaven's sake. Constance seemed busy enough at the oven, banging great pots. Bonnie was engrossed in some battered paperback luridly decorated with menstrual calendars, and seductively entitled *Have You Started Yet*? And Ally was brooding quietly over a chewed fingernail, worrying about whether or not he'd get to see Ned again before September. I was just stepping into the breach, trying to amuse Nance with that little problem.

"Listen," I said, when she began to look blank. "It's perfectly simple. I'll explain again." Gathering a bit of the cutlery round me, I built a bifurcated road between the water glasses and the butter dish. "There," I said. "That's the fork."

She was still looking blank. I pointed to my arrangement.

"No difficulty so far, I take it?" I asked patiently. "You do see the fork?"

"Which fork?"

"What do you mean, which fork?" I stabbed the table top. "This fork here."

Nancy said sullenly:

"There's four forks there. Which one do you mean?"

I looked down. We were at cross purposes. I'd built my fork in the road mostly from forks.

No need to court confusion. I reached out to harvest a few knives and spoons. Ally appeared totally indifferent to this annexation of his eating implements; but Bonnie reached out from behind her book to snatch hers back.

"'Scuse me. I'm *using* those."

"All right. No need to snap."

"No need to snatch."

"No need to bicker," said Constance, stirring.

I started off again.

"Now try to concentrate," I said to Nance. "There are two angels standing beside this fork."

"Which fork?"

"The fork in the road."

"Oh, that fork."

Children won't listen. Have you noticed that?

I kept my temper.

"As I was saying, there are two angels standing at this fork in the road. They look exactly the same. So do the roads, but one leads to heaven and the other to hell. One of the angels always tells the truth. The other always lies. You have to find the right road."

"The right road where?"

"To heaven, of course. Who'd want to go to hell?"

Constance muttered something over her boiling pots, and, like a fool, I asked: "What was that, Constance?" A more responsible parent might have had the self-control to answer, "Oh, nothing." But Constance, of course, repeated distinctly between gritted teeth: "I said that you might very well want to send someone else there."

Choosing to ignore this, I turned back to Nancy.

"You only get the chance to ask one question, mind. And all an angel can reply is 'yes' or 'no'. So what question should you ask?"

94

I sat back, waiting. It's a nice little problem. I've watched it keep whole tables of philosophers happy for hours.

"Well?" Nancy said. "What question should I ask?"

"You tell me."

"Why? You know the answer, don't you?"

"I do know one possible solution, yes."

"Then tell me."

"But you're supposed to work it out for yourself. That's the whole point."

"How can I? One of the angels lies, and no-one knows which!"

"That's what makes it such a nice problem."

Nancy just scowled. But when she heard Constance muttering "Bloody stupid!" in her pots, she made an effort out of filial loyalty.

"Let me think. I'd pick one of the angels and I would ask her —"

Bonnie lifted her head from her book for the first time.

"Angels aren't she," she said. "Angels are he."

"Not always," said Nancy. They started arguing at once, and it turned into quite a spirited little discussion, with even Ally's ears pricking up a bit, and Constance, of course, shoving in her opinion.

"Can we get back to the point, please?" I interrupted them all. "What question should you ask?"

Bonnie said irritably:

"You know. You tell us."

"You're supposed to work it out."

Silence. I can't claim I was expecting a sensible contribution from Constance. And Ally's hopeless, of course. But what do the girls do all day every day in school? Does no-one teach them how to *think*?

"Listen," I said. "It's perfectly simple. You choose one of the angels, point up one of the roads, and ask this question: "If I were to ask the other angel if this is the road to heaven, would he say 'Yes'?""

No-one responded. It was extraordinary. Constance began to serve. Ally inspected his scratches. Bonnie turned back to her book, and Nancy just looked at me vaguely across the table.

"Well?" I demanded. "What do you think?"

"Think?"

"Yes," I said. "Think. What do you think? It's clever, isn't it?"

"I don't know. I don't get it."

Was Einstein a father? Did he have to put up with this sort of thing at the table?

"Listen," I said again. "It's perfectly simple."

Constance slammed a full plate of steaming food down in front of me. Half of it shot off into my lap.

"Stop saying that, Olly!"

"Stop saying what?"

"'It's perfectly simple!'"

"But it is!" I spooned great heaps of beans out of my crotch back on to the plate. "Once you've been told the answer you could kick yourself for not working it out at once. If the angel's answer is 'no', then the road that you're pointing to has to be the road to heaven; and if he answers 'yes' it's the road to hell."

Nancy pointed a bean on her fork at me accusingly.

"How do you know?"

"Because it's *obvious*." I leaned across to explain. "Suppose, first of all, that it was the honest angel you happened to ask. Then he would quite truthfully tell you that the other angel would give you a dishonest answer to your question, and so 'yes' would mean 'no' and 'no' would mean 'yes'. Suppose, on the other hand, that you had chosen to ask the dishonest angel. Then he would falsely make out that the other angel would have given you the wrong answer. And so, again, 'yes' would mean 'no' and 'no' would have to mean 'yes'."

It could have been armistice morning. The silence was total. Then Constance said, a shade unpleasantly, "Oh, stands to reason, dunnit?" and Ally asked, mystified:

"Where's all my cutlery?"

Nancy reached out to slide my fork (his knife and spoon) across the table towards him.

Constance turned to Bonnie.

"Don't read at the table," she told her. "Especially not that."

She turned to Alasdair.

"And you can stop worrying about Ned."

"*Jawohl, mein Führer!*"

She turned to me.

"As for you, Olly. Do you think you could possibly stop thinking for one bloody meal?"

Stop thinking! Ally's quite right. Constance is a real Nazi by nature — wants to make everyone in the world bend to her will. Stop thinking. Silly cow. She was always saying that to me when we were married, I remember. It used to drive me mad. Thoughts aren't like water flowing from a tap. You can't just turn them off. Well, maybe idiots can. I certainly can't.

I'd have a go though, every now and again, just to please her. Sometimes I'd give it a try in the back garden on a summer's evening when I came out to be sociable. "You just can't relax there peacefully without thinking, can you?" she'd jeer, seeing me sitting there twitching. And so I'd really try, to prove her wrong. I'd stretch out flat on my back at her side on the grass, and stare up at the sky, and try to force my mind to empty. The sky's extraordinary when you're on your back. Strolling down streets or glancing out of windows you only get to see the thinnest rim of it. On your back you can see it all, the vast upturned bowl of it, stretching for miles and miles in peaceful blue, or hanging over you in dark bruisy colours, threatening to spill. I found the sensation astonishing every time, like slipping underwater suddenly into another world. I'd feel grass prickling beneath my skin, and hear the birds. Had they been singing all year, and I'd not noticed them? I'd feel air on my face and smell the lilac hanging over next door's fence. When I opened my eyes, I'd notice daisies for the first time since the year before, and find myself marvelling at their spread petals or their delicate pursed buds. I'd be amazed how clean and white they looked against our ragged grass. And when I lifted my head to look around, the sun would sail out in a thin silver slice from behind a cloud, and I'd be astonished by the length of the shadows.

It never lasted, though. It's not my style. Within minutes I'd be fretting about my plans for the coming term: wondering just how to bully that old fart Fletcher into forcing a few of the deadbeats at the top to take on their fair share of the seminar work, planning my courses so as to cut out hours of tedious preparation, trying to arrange things so I'd get just a little bit of time for my own work.

"You know, Constance, if I manage to get this paper on 'Objective Probability' finished by the end of October —"

"See! You're thinking!"

"I did stop for a bit. I heard the birds."

She's cackling away herself now, of course, like some great overgrown hen.

"Can't have been more than a minute!"

"It was enough."

Too right. How do these people who lie on beaches all day long do it? Don't they have brains? Are they incapable of getting bored? It has occurred to me from time to time that if I'd been more like one of them, it's possible my brother might be alive to this day. Part of me still thinks I might have seen Solly getting into difficulty in the water on that particular afternoon. After, there was this nagging image in the back of my mind of some sort of waving and splashing that hadn't seemed natural — that, looking back on it, hadn't seemed right. But what I saw wasn't enough to break through, as it were. Constance used to go wild at me when the children were little. I can still see her standing there, weighed down with shopping bags, her face contorted with rage. "For Christ's sake, Olly! Surely you must have heard the bloody scream (crash/rush of water/sudden hush)? You've got *ears*, haven't you? Weren't you *listening*?"

But I don't listen. I don't even look. In fact, I sometimes think I don't really live as other people do, as Constance does. I'm like a man who's on a train for life. He takes his seat, unwraps his sandwiches, and though he knows that what's on the other side of the glass — the stinging rain, thrashed trees and spinning leaves — makes up the real world, you ask him how it seems and he will tell you that, to him, it's just a background vision rushing past like, well, yes, of course, shadows on a cave wall. And that's what daily life is like to me. What's real is in my head. Constance complained it was impossible to understand the way my mind worked. But how could she start? There's only one way in, and, sadly for her, the sign above the door says "Abstract Thought'. Constance has never taken any interest in that.

"What have I never taken any interest in, Olly?"

Oh, God. Never mind. Brazen it out.

"You've never taken any interest in philosophy."

"Few people do."

She's certainly not going to get out of it that way.

"But we were married. That should have made a difference."

"I don't see why. You never took much of an interest in my mopping floors."

Oh, ho. Thin ice. I turn to Alasdair.

"What about Stella?"

"Ratbag? She took no interest in my work at all. I doubt if she could tell a blackcurrant from a deadly nightshade berry."

"That could prove useful," Constance said thoughtfully.

"Mu-*um!*" Nancy was shocked. "Killing is wrong."

"I don't know," argued Constance. "You ask your father. I expect he'd take much the same line with killing as he did with lying. What did you say about that, Olly? Have I got it right? Didn't you find yourself recoiling a little from the proposition that it was always totally morally indefensible?"

"Well, he would say that, wouldn't he?" said Bonnie. "After what happened last Christmas."

There was a little gasp. I turned to Nance. Her eyes had filled with tears. I'd had enough.

"Now listen," I said. "What the hell is all this that keeps coming up about last Christmas? I thought last Christmas was a great success. I had a good time. I thought everyone else did, too. I bought you all nice presents, didn't I? Even Ally. I helped wash up. I even took care of the house for a week when you went down to Granny's —"

"And you killed all the gerbils," Bonnie announced. *J'accuse!*

Fat little tears in Nancy's eyes spilled over slowly, and down, down, down. I saw Ally reach out for her and then, in some anguish of his own, hold back, presumably out of deference to me. Constance could have gathered her up, but she'd taken on Bonnie.

"Your father didn't *kill* them. It was an accident."

"Letting things die isn't an accident."

Sol's brain — salty and still.

"I did not let it die!"

Everyone stared.

"It?" Bonnie pointed the finger. "It was *them*! Six in the cage, there were. Four dead already by the time we got back, and the other two staggering about. And they died after!"

Bugger the fucking gerbils.

"I looked after your manky pets for you! I did them every morning — filled up their water dish and poked in their filthy bedding to check they still had food."

"See!" Constance snapped at Bonnie. "That's what I said! He didn't mean to starve them. It was an accident. He saw the sunflower seed shells lying about the bottom of the cage, and just assumed they still had plenty to eat."

"Eat your crusts! Eat your crusts! Can't have any more till you've eaten your crusts!"

Constance put an end to Bonnie's hysterical shrieks by seizing her shoulders and shaking her, hard.

"That's right!" she hissed in her face. "That's what he thought. Now get off his back, Bonnie. Leave him alone!"

"He could have looked!"

"He doesn't see!"

"What is he — blind? Or stupid?"

Nancy began to sob. Ally laid a great hand on her shoulder, then pushed her forward, gently, into my arms. She clung round me, making me feel like a tree trunk.

Constance said coldly to Bonnie:

"When you grow up, I hope you will try to be kinder to people."

"Like you?" scoffed Bonnie. "Do everyone a favour! One of your sort is enough for any house!"

Fetching the plaster down the walls, she slammed out.

Ally went after her. I couldn't face it. I sat with Nancy for a little while, till Constance led her off to wash her face. Then I slipped off upstairs. While I was sitting here, Constance sent up a cup of coffee via Alasdair.

"Sorry about all that."

I took the cup.

"Not your fault, Alasdair."

"No." He looked miserable. "Still, it's not easy."

"Difficult age, of course."

"Yes. Still —"

"And probably the wrong end of the month. Wasn't she reading a book on the topic just before supper?"

"I think she was, yes. Still —"

"Tell Constance thank you for the coffee, anyhow."

"Constance? Oh, right. Well, if there's anything —"

"Thanks, Ally."

Thanks, Ally. I can do without your sympathy. That's what I always hated most about this house, the sympathy that oozes all over you daily, eating away at your power, corroding your will. Poor Olly this, poor Olly that. Poor Olly nothing. Save your sympathy. I don't need understanding. I don't need help. Bonnie's quite right. Constance's kindness works like a noose she slips around your neck. It goes on, oh so gently, without your even noticing. And gently, gently, you are led away from all your hopes and dreams, all your ambitions. She'd cut your balls off with her sympathy if she could, and leave you as impotent as all the rest of the good family men she so admires.

Well, they underestimated me, her and her mother. I'm not a Hoover. I am King of Mars. I got away, where thousands wouldn't — put a whole ocean and half a continent between what was grudgingly offered and what was deserved. Given the choice, I wasn't going to stop and rot between one niggardly, cheese-paring sabbatical and the next. Offer the price — a bit of time to think — and you have got your man: Oliver Rosen. Give Constance her due, it was a battle royal. She was appalled the day I brought home that letter, spotted at once in the office mailbox as much for my instantaneous lifting of spirits as for its brash American stamp, bright signpost out of hell. She is by no means daft, my former wife. She knew what was at stake right from the start. She knew my views on crumbling British universities. And she knew precisely what I thought of my colleagues. In this respect, at least, she knew my mind.

Constance fought like a ferret. But I won.

CHAPTER
FIVE

You can barely get into the kitchen before she pounces.

"How far have you got?"

"Chicago."

"Oh, yes?"

She's waiting for more. I tried to make it back to the safety of the door. But:

"What have you written so far?"

"Not very much."

"Liar. That's quite a wodge you're clutching, Olly. Read some out."

"'And, as before, the relation 'A is forced by the condition p' is expressed as a first-order condition A' (p).'"

"Not that bit. The first line."

Is she a witch?

"You're not going to like this very much, Constance."

"Oh, go on. Be brave, Olly. Read it out."

"'The year of my move to Chicago —'"

"*Your* move?" The knife stalls with dramatic effect mid chop-chop-chop. "Who did the work? Who packed everyone's boxes?"

Oh, God. Can't she see that I'm busy? Can't she see that I simply don't have time to break off and run through a repeat performance of Our Marriage Show, just because she's bored with chopping cabbage?

"Is that the doorbell?"

"No. No it isn't. Go on, Oliver. The year of your move to Chicago . . . ?"

"'The year of my move to Chicago was chiefly notable for —'"

Chop-chop-chop-chop. She looks cheerful enough, but I'm not fooled. Constance is Old Moore's spiritual daughter. Which of the horrors of that year is foremost in her mind? The appalling upheaval? The miscarriage that, coupled with my unfamiliarity with a new medical system, almost led to disaster? My brother's vanishing act? Her father's breakdown?

"'Was chiefly notable for . . . ?'"

"Constance, I'm in the middle of it. Must I stop?"

"Just one teensy-weensy sentence, Oliver. Just so I get the drift." Chop-chop. "Please. Pretty, pretty please. I am cooking your lunch . . ."

Checkmate.

"Promise you won't throw coleslaw at me."

"Promise."

"'The year of my move to Chicago was chiefly notable for the fact that I finally found myself breaking away from the subjectivist tradition to the extent of allowing objective probabilities to figure in . . .'"

If I am faltering it is because the chopping knife has suddenly gone deathly still.

"Please, Constance. Don't. Throw the whole bloody cabbage at me, if you must. But just don't start up. I simply couldn't stand it."

106

There is the little pause that you'd expect. And then: "Oh, all right, Olly. Off you go."

And off I went. Women are strange to begin with. And marriage makes them stranger. But with divorce it seems to me a goodly number of them must take leave of their senses. Who but a former wife would ever let you off the hook like that, as blithely and easily as she'd pinned you on?

She may have done the work and packed all the boxes, but it was terrible all round.

"Constance, for God's sake stop bothering with that. They won't mind if they find a few apple cores under the bed."

Out comes the rental agreement, object of implacable hatred and scorn. "Leave clean all walls, woodwork, skirting boards, tiles, windows, floors, fixtures and electrical switch-plates . . ." Who would have thought there could be so much to a house? It had more nerve-endings than I did. The problems were legion. What should we do with the cat? The yoghurt culture on the kitchen window sill? The half-eaten subscription to *Private Eye*? The annual delivery of cut-price summer coal? Sometimes I'd find her, shadow-eyed with strain, crouched in the corner of a darkening room, brooding.

"My future's stopping. I can feel it stop. We're all being sacrificed for you, Olly. I don't even bother to look at the job pages in the paper any longer. Nancy has had to give up her part in the nursery-school play. And all Bonnie's mates are on the lookout for new best friends, now that they've realized we'll be away for two whole years. Our lives are grinding to a halt for you."

"Oh, come on, Constance. You might like it there."

"I like it here."

Her eyes won't meet mine. They roam round and round the room, storing the memory of it to take along with us, with all the boxes and bags, into our exile. Women will always make bad refugees. Home's where the heart is, and their hearts are home. Until the move to Chicago, I think I must have assumed quite automatically that I and my behaviour were the two chief determinants of whether Constance stayed married to me. There'd been no warning that love might be conditional on her continuing to thrive around familiar people, places and things. Over the years, Constance had loved me for better and worse, for richer and poorer (though, as with most couples, it was the other way round) and, if you count one singularly prolonged attack of viral flu, in sickness and in health. How were the two of us supposed to guess the one insuperable hurdle would prove to be "at home and overseas"?

"It will make a nice change for you and the children."

"Me and the children don't like change."

True. As soon as the first faint shadow of upheaval fell across the household, Nancy began to cling, Bonnie to whine. The children picked up their unease directly from their mother, for whom, so far as I can make out, Change is synonymous with Mortal Threat. What little personal equilibrium Constance possesses has always been principally sustained by steady routine. The more each of her days mirrors the one before, the happier she is. She sinks herself into the rhythms of each day as others sink themselves in welcoming bath water. She knows the foibles and preferences of everything around her. "Don't water that any more, Nancy. Pinks hate to get their feet wet." And over the years she's even come to treat the house as if it were some huge and sentient organic entity, with its own patterns and habits. "That light will move out of your eyes in a minute." "The post will be here soon." "You must be early. The boiler hasn't switched itself on yet." "Where's the cat? On the front wall, I should think. Or, if the sun's gone in, try Bonnie's bed."

It's a huge body of knowledge to master. It must take time. Then there's the provenance and history of every single object in the house, including the contents of cupboards and wardrobes, and most of the plants in the garden. Living with Constance is like "Antiques Roadshow". "Those? Those aren't our shells from France. Our shells from France are in that smelly glass jar on the shelf in the bathroom. Those are just some old shells Stringbean picked up on Salcey beach and hasn't bothered to take home."

To me, it's just "shells", or "chair". Or, at the very most, "new chair". ("Not *new,* Olly. It's been sitting there for weeks. Aunty Grace dumped it on my mother at Bertha's funeral, but she has nowhere to put it. The bloody thing's falling apart but it's 'sentimental'. If we don't want it, we're to give it back.")

I listen, nod, even smile. But I don't register. Point to the object under discussion next week, and it will have reverted in my mind to simple "chair". Constance's definition, on the other hand, will have developed all manner of extraordinary and vivid accretions. "Poor

Nancy trapped her finger down the back of it yesterday. The thing's a death trap. I'll have to buy some wood glue and get it fixed. And I bet Aunty Grace was fibbing about the woodworm holes just to get rid of the damn thing. I bet there are hundreds of the little buggers in there, still in the pink of health, chomping away. They'll be out for day trips soon, noshing their way through our floorboards. Old people are so selfish. They'll lie through their false teeth to get their way."

I tell you, if my brain got clogged up with this sort of domestic detritus, I'd willingly take a knife and slit my throat. Some people might have been grateful to be offered the chance to move away from everything and everyone that cluttered up their life, and start anew.

Not Constance. Oh, not her.

"What do you take me for, Olly? A bloody immigrant?" The rings around her eyes were darkening — always a bad sign. "Do I look starving? Persecuted? Displaced by war?"

"For God's sake, Constance —"

"Don't 'For God's sake, Constance' me, Olly! Why should I be sweet and reasonable and cooperative about packing up my whole life and moving halfway across the bloody world?"

"Because we're married and I hate it here!"

There go the dishes she's packing. Smash! Bang! Crash! No wonder both our children are nervous wrecks.

"How *dare* you? You have a home here! You have us. You have three meals a day."

"And a crappy job!"

"Most people have crappy jobs."

"I'm not most people."

"You're certainly not! You have all those bloody enormous university holidays, and even in term time you get two clear days a week!"

"I should get four! If that old fool Fletcher had either the vision or the guts to force some of his fossil friends to pick up their fair share of the teaching load, I might have time to *think*."

I must sound desperate. Her tone is softening.

"You could try for another research job, Olly. You never know. You might be lucky next time."

Take care now, Revilo Nesor. Here comes the sympathy. Chin up.

"Luck has nothing whatsoever to do with who is appointed to research positions, Constance. The Oxford system isn't a lottery, you know. I didn't get that fellowship for a reason, and the reason was that somebody from the college gave it to somebody else from the college — someone whose only claim to fame is going to be that he once got a job I didn't get!"

Well, that's at least seen off the sympathy.

"Oh, you! You! Fucking you, you, you!" With complete disregard for the terms of the rental agreement, she's kicking bits of shattered cereal bowl out of sight under the oven and the fridge. "What about the children? What about me? I know you, Olly. You say it will be two years. But then it'll be two more. Then two more." She tums to point the finger and send the message loud and clear. "Well, I warn you, Olly. If I don't like it I am coming back, and I can tell you right now that I'm not going to like it!"

She didn't like it. She wasn't miserable about it, I'll give her that. I thought, in fact, she was a sight more cheerful through each day than she'd been back in Britain. But that might have been a result of the generous child-care provision available locally. In my opinion, Constance has always been better for a little bit of time to herself every day.

I think the fairest way of describing what happened is that, from the moment she set foot on foreign soil, she traded Housewife's Depression for Traveller's Spite. She noticed everything, took for mere passing accident what she might have quite liked had it turned up at home, and made a point of despising the rest. And, like her famous precursor, de Tocqueville, she saved her deadly fire for the soft targets.

"Why do they talk so slowly? Are they brain-damaged?"

"Of course they're not brain-damaged, Constance. How could they all be brain-damaged?"

"They're none of them born naturally, you know. They have stuff injected in them to start the birth off, and stop the pain, and speed the contractions up, and slow them down, and dry up the milk, and contract the uterus. They have dozens of injections."

"So?"

"So maybe the stuff gets in their brains."

"Constance, it's cultural, not physical. They just talk more slowly."

"It's not just how slowly they talk, Olly. It's what they say. They're always telling you things you already know. They're always saying things like: "Of course, our political system differs in some respects from your own. You have a Prime Minister, and we have a President. You have the Houses of Parliament, and we have a Senate and a House of Representatives. And our constitution is not the same as yours —'"

"They're only trying to be helpful."

"I wouldn't mind except, what with them talking so slowly . . ."

"I'm sure you'll get used to it."

"I don't think I will. You see, they don't speak normally, either."

"What do you mean, they don't speak normally?"

"I mean they only use a few words, and they use them over and over like au pairs and drunks. You take this morning. I turned up at the day-care centre in time to watch the end of that game where you try and organize yourself two minutes' peace by sending all the children off to find something. They were drifting back with all sorts of things: stones, pebbles, flints, lumps of masonry, handfuls of filthy gravel. One of them was even staggering back with a bloody great boulder in her arms. And the lady who runs the playgroup called all of them 'rocks'."

"Be fair, Constance. A rock is probably what she sent them out to find."

"Maybe it is. But she said the same thing to every single one of them. She said: 'That is certainly a wonderful rock.' Eight times in a row she said it. She *must* be brain-damaged. I'd have gone mad."

"You wouldn't take a job in a day-care centre."

"Not having to say it, Olly. Having to *listen*."

"Nancy seems happy enough."

"She does, doesn't she?" Constance looked anxious. And perhaps it was some trace memory of herself reaching, cursing with pain, for more gas and air, that caused her to abandon her brain-damage theory, and replace it the very next evening with another.

"I know why they all talk so slowly. It's all these nice nurseries. Americans are raised by people who are comparatively well-paid and work in pleasant conditions, and generally enjoy the company of small children."

"What difference does that make?"

"Well, it's not normal."

I knew exactly what she meant. I'm British too. But I have spent my life in universities. And so, on behalf of a couple of other departments further along the corridor or up the lift, I felt obliged to ask "What's normal?" and face her frankly unbelieving stare.

"Oh, you know, Olly! Don't act so bloody dense. Normal is getting pissed off with picking the same stupid toys off the floor over and over again, day after day. Normal is snarling at poor little tired weeping toddlers, and using methods you swore you'd never use like bribery and threats and blackmail, just to try and stay sane. Normal is hitting the gin bottle straight after tea-time, and hearing yourself sound just like your own mother, and pulling the phone cord round corners so you can squat in the cupboard at the bottom of the stairs moaning to your last stay-at-home-with-the-children friend about how cheesed off you are, and how it's

114

another three years before anyone gets to the top of the waiting list for nursery, and how, if they're not careful, you're going to strangle them. Normal is creeping out of the cupboard to find they've come back from wherever you sent them so as not to bash them up, and have been standing right on the other side of the door listening to every word you said." She spread her hands. "No wonder British children make a bit of an effort to be clever and amusing, and talk fast and impress you with brand new words you never heard them use before like 'pebble' and 'boulder'. Poor little sods probably think their lives are at stake."

It's an interesting hypothesis. And, as with the great majority of Constance's theories, there may be more to it than meets the eye. Personally, I have learned not to scoff too loudly or too soon about any of Constance's *ex cathedra* pronouncements. I was caught out on the demerits of fluorescent lighting ("It may be cheap, Olly, but all that horrid glare and flickering can't be good for you"), sunbeds ("Bet they turn out to cause cancer"), and the personal integrity of the Co-op milkman ("Didn't I tell you he was trying it on?"). If I were a betting man I'd put money on Constance, most particularly *vis-à-vis* one or two of her current but so far unproven theories concerning the statistical link between susceptibility to cancer and infrequency of orgasm, the role of language laboratories in schools ("Bloody useless!"), and the long-term political prospects of Gerald Kaufman. If past form is anything to go on at all, I'd rake in some sizeable lump sums to see me through the coming years.

The coming years . . . And as the first two did stretch into four, then six, the very thought of these became a matter of dissension between us, a rift in the marriage opening so wide that each of us could stand on our own bank and look down at what lay seething in the chasm between us: her permanent dissatisfaction — or mine.

I loved America. It was, for me, truly a New Found Land. A country filled with people as prodigal with goodwill as with food, who remembered your name from one meeting to another, and didn't set their faces almost imperceptibly against the way you ate, or spoke, or got straight to the point. A land of secretaries willing to type, generous with paper clips, quick to be helpful. A system of universities in which, for every black or woman or hispanic employed in large part because of a policy of quotas, there were at least a dozen white male idiots weeded out because of the policy of reading applicants' work. All very different from at home, where I recall with bitter clarity an appointment of signal importance in which, although not invited to become a member of the Admissions Committee, I was, so far as I could establish, the only philosopher who actually bothered to look at what the people on the shortlist had written. My remonstrations at the hiring of a charlatan went all the way up to the Senate, to much departmental embarrassment but no avail. He was a pleasant enough fellow — held his knife correctly, spoke very nicely, too. But it's small wonder that when I think back to the names most frequently tossed about in pubs and coffee bars twenty years ago (who's bright, who's sound, who's working on something rather interesting, who's good to talk to) none of them are still here. If I wanted someone to talk to this summer, I'd have to fly to Australia, or go home.

And it is home now. I like the enormous fridges, and the workmen who turn up exactly at the time they said they would, and roads so straight and wide that even I could pass the driving test. I like working in a meritocracy. If it were not for Constance's ever-burgeoning demands on behalf of the children, I'd probably be indifferent to my own frequent increments of salary on the grounds of exceptional academic merit; but I love watching Dupinberry waste away, emolumentally speaking, on little more than the salary he was earning thirteen years ago, when he was inadvertently offered tenure. In Britain, he'd have the professorship by now.

Everyone works here. That's another thing I like. Those who can, get the research time. Those who can't, teach *Introduction to Logic*. Even Dupinberry gets packed off regularly to Reform Seminar, forced practically at torn-up contract point to read his students' scathing reports, and watch himself on in-house video, droning his way through his vacuous and ill-considered lectures. Give the administration their due, they may wear funny suits and have degrees in things like History of Sport, but they at least do their energetic best to rid the system of freeloaders and incompetents. It's a pity the same thing hasn't happened in Britain where, whether through miscalculation or malign intent, the only obvious effect of the prolonged and painful academic squeeze is that there are no longer cushy berths for everyone. Between the gifted and the greasy-polers, the time-servers and brown-tonguers and dead wood, somebody had to go. It's just a pity that those who frittered their energies away on intellectual effort hadn't time to make footholds, and fell off first.

Still, not my problem now. I say what I think when anybody asks, but otherwise (and especially since that unpleasant evening during the Third Leamington Conference) I've tended to keep off the topic of Philosophy in Britain. If they prefer to treat the post-mortem purely as a family matter, that's their affair. I'm safely out. I think the taxpayer is entitled to resent the fact that the returns I have to offer on a costly education are benefiting those who didn't pay for it; but in this I am only one of hundreds of thousands of academics and engineers, scientists and nurses. Waiting around in Britain for a state of affairs in which you can simply do what you've been trained to do, and do it well, is a bit like waiting for lunchtime in this house. By the time it arrives — was that The Great Shout Up The Stairs at last? — you will have grown a beard down to your feet.

Excuse me, Olly. I am *using* these pillowcases. It was all right when you were stuffing your papers in the old Noddy one. I didn't even mind when you spilled over into the Victoria Plums. But now your great work of art is overflowing into the matching florals, I have to ask you to move out again. Can't you shove it all in something that nobody uses? How about one of the sleeping bags? Or a nice big ticking mattress cover. I'm trying to run this household, and it's not easy when all my clean laundry keeps getting stuffed to the gills with reams of autobiographical self-analysis, and warnings about nurses growing beards.

And I'm sorry I didn't want to live in America for ever and ever, causing you such inconvenience. I didn't despise it all, either, as you very well know. Some things were wonderful. I loved not having to carry my own groceries. It was quite lovely to be trusted to take out more than three miserable library books at any one time. And I particularly enjoyed being treated for once as a real human being as opposed to a crummy and downtrodden British wife. (Farewell to "Wives invited? Gosh, yes, Oliver. We shall need all the help with the teas we can get!")

I think America's *better*, if you must know. It's just I like it here. You scoff at my knowing what day the fish van comes and where the cat sleeps as if I were some kind of neurotic pea-brain, but there is more to it than that, the same way there's more to philosophy than Bertrand Russell's granny's "What is mind, dear? No matter. What is matter? Never mind." My mental life's as rich as yours, mate. It's just different. You dig some tattered old rag out of that duster box. Go on. Pick one out. Any one at all. Hold it up so I can see it. I'll tell you not only what it was, but where it came from, who wore it first, and whether it held out long enough to be a hand-me-down. I'll tell you exactly how the child looked when she was wearing it, what she could and couldn't do at that age, which stuffed animal she loved the most, and some of the funny little things she used to say. I'll even

119

tell you exactly how I felt the day I peeled it off her for the last time, and cut it up into dusters. As long as you've been a philosopher, I've been the qualified historian of this house and all its occupants. You wouldn't want to change fields, would you? Well, stuff you, Olly. Neither did I.

And what's so wrong with wanting to know which day is early closing at the shops, and what time the water gets hot? Most people live that way. Life works out smoother. Not knowing things is *your* speciality, not mine. You don't mind it. You even like it. The watchwords of your profession are Doubt and Uncertainty. If you don't know something, you can ask a bloody great Airy-Fairy Question about it. There's nothing you lot like more than that!

Well, I don't care for not knowing. If I slip up — over what day it is, or what's the time, or whether the boiler's supposed to be on yet — something real always goes wrong. Someone misses swimming for the third time in a row and gets dropped from the team, or there's no food in for supper, or I end up having to wash my hair in cold water. I like to get things right. I'm not like you, offered an office and a title, and paid to sit about wondering. My little certainties are important to me. If I manage to back several of the poor, pathetic little things up, end to end, all in one day, I might get five whole minutes to read the paper!

That's what I can't stand about you philosophers, Olly. You're all so fucking lofty. You act like there's something on the horizon that only you can see, and recognize, and even begin to describe. You think the rest of us are blind to the great mysteries of existence. You think that we're just insensible clods, stamping around obsessed with trivia like getting in more lavatory paper, and fixing the Hoover, and trying to remember whether it was lemon sole with flaked almonds the Warrens had last time they came round for supper. I think you think I don't like philosophy simply because it's useless. Well, you're wrong. I'm not stupid. I know we don't need philosophy any more than we need art or music, and we need it just as much as we need those. I don't want to live on potatoes. I am not *thick*. Do you want to know something, Olly? It's not what you do. It's the bloody way that you do it. What I can't stand about your philosophy is all the rage and power and intensity that ends up being sucked into it. You burst out of your study, possessed with energy, practically beating your chest. "This is brilliant, Constance. Quite brilliant! So far it is the best thing I've done, I know!" But everyone round you is a bloody limp rag. You've written the whole thing at their expense. You've never noticed me (except at bedtime), snarled at the children, trodden on the cat. Your mind raced all night, so you slept in the mornings. And everyone ended up creeping about, keeping their voices down, shutting doors quietly — and endlessly, endlessly *guilty*. How did we come to feel as if we were forever dragging you down? As if, if we weren't hanging round you, you could fly? Honestly, the day I interrupted you to tell you those roof timbers were caving in over Bonnie's bedroom, I actually felt mean. Can you believe that? We really drained your crystals, didn't we? We really wasted your time. I realized one fine day that absolutely everything I like in the world — reading the papers, cuddling babies, caring for animals — is a distraction for you, another stupid thing to be circumvented before you can get back to your passion: what's in your head. You fellows shouldn't get married. I've browsed through old Bertie's autobiography often enough, watching the sprouts. I know what I'm talking about. "I then rode away on my bicycle, and with that my first marriage came to an end." How does that rate for sensitivity? I'll tell you, Olly. It rates *low*.

Let's hope the children haven't inherited any of your pesky genius. I certainly won't be making any effort to cultivate it. In fact, I'd much prefer to stamp it out. There's only room for one in any family, and all the rest need a bloody support group. I ought to start one for the Wives of Important Philosophers (call it WIMPS) — except they're all abroad. How about widening the membership to include everyone in any family tied to a Clever Person? They share a common problem. Only one person is allowed to build their life, while all the rest have to wait, and adapt, fit in, defer, make do. I could produce a little handbook. *Advice to the Innocent Beginner:* Your first trip abroad. Make sure you fuck this one up properly. Whatever you do, don't go along gracefully with your spouse, cheerfully moving wherever he suggests, finding new friends, involving yourself in new projects, making sure to stay busy and cheerful, and helping your children adapt. Because, if you do, you will have only your stupid self to blame when he points out your obvious capabilities, and uses them as evidence against you when he decides he wants to move again — and again — and again — and again.

Choice of guilts, ladies: fuck up your husband's career, or yourself and the children. You've seen those giant Pickfords vans thundering up and down the motorways. You and your kids have lost enough best friends. We live in dangerous times. Only a very few escape the six o'clock rattle of the key in the lock, and the heart-stopping cry: "I say, Angela! Listen to this. There's a bit of a reshuffle going on at Head Office, and Higgins actually suggested over lunch today . . ."

What about you? Are you already leaping to your feet, laying aside the curtains you've just this minute finished hemming to the exact right length for the windows? "Oh, splendid, darling! I can always hem them again!" Good. You are obviously the right sort to marry a Clever Person. The rest of you, take care, read this booklet, and don't say a word till you've seen your solicitor.

Yes, yes. I admit it. I had had enough. I was homesick. I came home. Oh, I made the usual excuses: claimed that I found it impossible to live indefinitely in a country in which both pebbles and boulders are referred to as "rocks", graduate students say things like "That's *your* reality", and even the grown-ups still believe in God. But, really, I hadn't wanted to go in the first place, and didn't see why I should stay. But I still feel bitter about it, Oliver, the way our move to America ended up being treated in family mythology as if it were simply some insignificant part of a natural progression, but my coming back was a Great Big Decision. I don't think that was fair. Nor do I think it was very chivalrous of you to take advantage of the geography of the matter to leave all your colleagues with the impression that *I* had left *you*. As my mother rather tartly pointed out when she came to pick me and the children up from the airport, some people are old enough to remember when it was always the gentleman who left . . .

CHAPTER
SIX

"Is there anything in that teapot?"

"Yes. I filled it with sump oil from next door's Toyota."

I should never have risked coming down. She's in one of her moods.

"Girls all right?"

"I think so. This huge nasty black thing swooped down and pecked out both of Nancy's eyes, but the ambulance men took her off, so it's all quiet now."

A real mood. I'd take a quick peep at the calendar, except that the merest glance of mine in that direction now would be enough to unhinge her. Cotton-wool tactic time, I think.

"Managing, are you?"

"Oh, yes. I lost my head for a moment earlier, and drank a pint of weed-killer. But I'm fine now."

She'll go through the bottom of that pan in a minute. Why is she cooking woollies anyway? Has she gone mad?

Here it comes.

"Oliver, can you stir, please? Just for a moment?"

Oh, no. Oh, no, no, no. I am afraid I am not having that, whichever week we're in. She cannot have it both ways. Either we are married, or we are not. And we are not.

"Where's Ally, then?"

Watch out, pan.

"Over at Ratbag's."

Oh, ho. I see.

"No, you do *not*!"

I didn't even say it. For God's sake. I didn't even open my mouth.

It's worked, though, hasn't it? Because I so much as had the temerity to think it, quietly, to myself, I end up having to take the wooden spoon from her, and she ends up lolling on a kitchen chair, leisurely pulling on socks. Well, she'd bloody well better not be planning to abandon me. I can't stand here stirring all day. I'm in the middle of working.

"Don't taste that, Olly. It'll stain your teeth."

At least she's softening a bit. (Can't be the worst week.)

"What is this, anyway?"

"Dye."

"*Dye*?"

"It's Nancy's Brownie uniform. I only just bought it, and now she's moving up to Guides. I'm trying to dye it blue."

"Are my teeth blue? Quick, Constance! Come and have a look at them! Have all my teeth gone blue?"

"Don't panic, Olly."

I must say, she certainly takes her time, finishing adjusting her woolly socks just so, and hauling on her wellies, before she even bothers to stroll across and check. And even then all she does is reach out and lift my upper lip, as if I were some sort of old horse she was thinking of buying.

126

"Please don't do that."

"You're all right. You're not blue. I'll slip a pinny round you, though. Just to be safe."

"Constance, I am not stopping. I am working."

Before I can even move, she's slid the pinafore over my head and got her octopus arms round my waist, knotting me firmly.

"Just for a minute, Olly."

And she is out the back door.

Explain to me, someone, please, how things work out this way. How is it that, at the end of a marriage, everything you quite liked about the relationship disappears instantly as if by magic, and all the little things you secretly loathed persist to haunt you down the coming years? How come my wishes are still being ignored? Why am I standing here stirring? I did think that when I was so summarily surfed out of the job of being Constance's husband, there would be compensations. I might at least be offered the prerogatives of the lodger. (That I had anyway slipped into this role was, after all, the gist of Constance's justification for the Great Swap-About.) Lodgers don't have to stir. Lodgers don't find themselves strapped into pinnies at the stove, spooning little Brownie frocks round pots with one hand and desperately trying to write with the other. Where's she gone, anyway? Why is she paddling about in the garden in all this rain? Can I smell burn—? Christ Almighty! Nancy will be so upset. Can Constance patch char holes? Oh, I expect so. Women can do anything that bloody suits them.

Whereas I — I am trammelled by the patterns of the past. Things in this house have always been like this. "Oh, Olly. Please. It's only for a moment." The little deadlines that I set myself quickly become a sick joke. My routines go to hell. Everything I try to think about ends in confusion. My wits scatter over battlefields of domestic detritus. My inner forces all end up in rout. If I were to leaf back to the last sentence I wrote before this little interruption she's brewed, it would look as meaningless as hieroglyphics. I cannot work in this house. It is impossible. And there's no need even to glance in the direction of the calendar. It makes no difference. The Curse of Constance lies upon this house the whole month through, and God help anyone who wants to think.

Mind you, the family is the death of abstract thought. (Those who have feared the family has no role left in present-day society may take their comfort here: it does for work.) Constance goes slopping round the house day after day, distracting me with dusters and mops and worries about Bonnie's appalling education. I give her the evil eye. She gives it back. Eventually our horns lock. This morning, for example. I was lying peacefully in my bed when she came through the door without even knocking.

"Don't wake up, Olly," she said loudly and clearly, though it was evident to anyone who took the trouble to look that my eyes, if not my ears, were firmly closed. "I'm only looking for something. I won't be a moment."

This moment stretched into a seemingly endless thudding and scrabbling. I knew only too well that if she didn't find what she was looking for pretty sharpish, she'd get too bored to stay quiet. Constance is far too intelligent to make a good housewife. And, sure enough, while she was slamming the drawers of the chest in and out, one by one, rooting through innards, she started addressing herself in the mirror above in one of her Channel Four documentary imitations. "To the casual observer," she said, "what you see behind me now on your television screens may appear to be nothing more than a sleeping lump in a bed. Nothing could be further from the truth. What is in fact the case is that an extraordinarily agile and versatile mind has sprung to life at the expense of the body that nurtures it. This is not merely a warm bed for sleeping in. It is a hotbed of ideas —"

"And the idea," I interrupted, opening one baleful eye, "is to get back to sleep."

(She can go on for hours if you don't stop her.)

The children are just as much trouble. When Ally was whistling beneath my window this morning, mulching his flowerpots, I moved down to the empty sitting room. I'd only been there a few minutes when Bonnie wandered in, stared at me watching the blank television screen while having a private little think about the nature of necessity, and then switched the bloody thing on.

"Must you watch *now*?"

"Now's when it's on."

Since this seemed furnished in the spirit of conclusive argument, I changed my ground.

"Please use the earpiece. I am working."

Grumbling, she picked just sufficient flex out of the tangled lump tying like a bleached dog turd on the floor to screw one end on the television, and the other in her ear.

"Another three feet of flex, please, or you'll ruin your eyes."

(I am a good father. I do try. I try.)

I shifted my back against whatever flickering idiocy she was watching, and tried to chase my train of thought.

Then:

Thunk.

Thunk.

She was banging her feet together on the carpet.

Thunk.

"Could you please stop that?"

"Stop what?"

"That thing you're doing with your feet."

"What thing?"

"That thunk."

"I'm not thunking."

She was quite right, of course. In order to enter into the discussion, she had, temporarily, given up thunking.

Thunk.

Thunk.

"There. That is exactly what I mean. That thunking. Will you please stop that?"

"You mean this?"

Thunk.

"Yes."

"What's wrong with that?"

"Nothing. It's just driving me mad. So stop it, please."

There was a moment's silence, then:

Thunk.

Oh, yes. Show me a family man, and I'll show you a hamstrung thinker. It's all these feelings that do it. They suck you down. They have the power to sponge out thought as easily as a magnet can wipe a disc. You have to be careful. If you want to get on with anything serious, you simply can't afford to keep giving them house-room. You have to take very great care to fence yourself in.

And then, of course, the accusations come flying. "You are insensitive. You are a clod. You have no bloody feelings at all." Where do people like Constance pick up their certainties so cheap? Where do they get the gall to go round wearing their threadbare assumptions for all the world as if they were the rich and venerable robes of impartial moral judgement? I do have feelings. I am not a clod. I may not come out of exactly the same box as Constance, but I am none the worse for that. Where's Constance's way of living ever got her, that's what I'd like to know. I have my work, my answers, my philosophy. What will she have? A fuller life? More people snivelling round her grave? Bully for her. I'll choose my own way, thanks. No-one can live two lives, and I picked mine.

I can remember when, too. It was a summer's morning, just like this. August the something — and my mother's birthday, so it seemed, for up the stairs it all came suddenly in the usual turmoil: her howls of distress and outrage, the penetrating background grind of his self-serving explanations, doors banging as brother after

131

brother went to ground. I can still hear the shrieking in my ears. "Nothing? Nothing at all? Not from anyone? Nothing? *Nothing*?"

Who came to her? Surely somebody came. It would be Solly, probably. Or Joe. Too late to ask now. No-one left. All I have is a memory of the rough underside of desk pressing against my legs, and the pressure of my fingers hard in my ears as I leaned over, blotting them all out once and for all, and tackled the first exercise starred for difficulty in Tarquel's magnificent *Introduction to Logic*. How old was I? Thirteen? Fourteen? A time to come of age. An age to choose.

Not that there was much in it — the choice, I mean. Always, when I've seen people like Constance and Ally fooling about, taking life lightly, I've known that way of living has never for me been a serious option. If I am honest I must face the fact that, for all the morning of my mother's birthday stands out in memory, I can't remember back to any time I didn't know I'd have to make myself an acolyte to all the possibilities waiting inside me. Those years in school I wasn't simply sitting there pretending to be King of Mars. I felt the mantle around my shoulders. And, when I search my conscience, I also know that there was no simple, self-protective metamorphosis taking place in me the day my mother howled like an animal in a trap, imprinting the communal negligence on all our minds. It was, rather, calm descending. A sudden ineradicable certainty that, for me, there was only one way to go; and since, in the end, I'd have to ignore all the emotional boilings to get there, I might as well start doing that now.

132

And I know what I'm missing. I'm not, as even Constance will admit, one of the great impoverished army of the repressed. I could, if I chose, change tack overnight — forsake philosophy and let the other side of me out into the daylight. Burn all the calendars, unplug the clocks, and *live* my days instead of simply using the bricks of them, the hours, to build a structure in another world. I'd feel as deeply as, these days, I think. And so it helps to keep the barriers high. And that's one of the things I have against Constance. To me she's always been, unwittingly, a source of strain. Like some insensitive tart touting for custom under a hermit's window, she is a vivid and infuriating reminder of joys left behind, and things so much time was spent burying. Frankly, I've always found people who come over strong a little hard to take. Toddlers. My colleagues' bright young second wives. Constance's mother. I don't like too much life thrust down my throat. I think that's why theatres annoy me. I do dislike theatres. I find them so disturbing, all that vitality pulsing away on bare boards. I don't mind books. Don't mind books at all. You can, at least, always put a book down. Besides, I only ever read the very best, and so I know whoever wrote them more than likely had a life like mine, stymied and circumscribed and drained to a purpose. Songs with words I avoid. They conjure feelings that can knock you sideways with the force of blows. It can take hours to settle after a song, so I'll have truck only with pure music now. And that, I find, works like a talisman to keep me on the path. I play each night. I listen every day. Oh, they sweep over me, these cadences of total purity. My mind's not closed to what they have to say. I hear the love, the anguish, loss, desire. But it's not pinned to life — phones that don't ring, loves that won't last. It's music to paint a portrait of my life as well. The soaring phrases can evoke the certainties I've struggled to find, the glorious arching beauties of my work —

My work . . . Oh, God. Where *is* she? Surely this Brownie frock is cooked by now. Why doesn't she come back? It's not as if I have time to fritter. Already this whole bloody summer is almost gone, and if that thing up there isn't finished by the time I fly out, I'll never come back to it. There are far too many other things to be done. It's my own fault. I should never have allowed myself to be seduced into accepting Otto Fairbairn's ridiculous offer. This sort of writing's for the gaga — or for the seriously in debt. If I hadn't lashed out on the Steinway I could have paid off his flock of third-rate intellectual gannets, and spent the summer doing something worthwhile.

If I'd been permitted to get round to doing anything. At least, from the sound of things outside the back door, Constance is on the way back. Does Freedom ring?

No.

"Olly, I can't get my boots off. Give us a hand."

"I'm busy stirring, Constance."

She is impervious to irony when it suits her.

"I'll stir. You tug the boots."

She's taking giant strides across the floor, no doubt to save on mopping later.

"What did you go out for anyhow, in all this wet?"

In answer, she holds a large fruit punnet triumphantly high.

"Blackcurrants?"

"Deadly nightshade."

"How on earth are you planning to get her to eat them?"

Constance dissolves in glee. It is a little game that she and Ally often play. I've not joined in before, though I have heard them at it often enough: "There's the 31 bus." "But she never crosses the road here." "Is that the noon gun?" "Yes, but how shall we get her to stand in front of it?" The two of them are really quite childish. And I expect that, out of my hearing, they play the game on my account as well. Maybe I should check out this sudden passion for poisonous fruit . . .

"These deadly nightshade berries, Constance. Why have you picked them? Should I be worrying?"

She lays her hand heavily on my head to steady herself just the way Nancy does as I grovel at her feet to pull off her boots.

"Constance?"

She's peering, quite distracted, in the pot.

"Don't fret, Olly. No-one is out to poison you. It's just that Ally's gone round to try and spring Ned for the afternoon, and Ned's an outdoorsman and a great berry eater."

I am appalled. Frankly appalled. Has neither of them any sense of responsibility at all?

"You should have asked me, Constance. I could have uprooted the entire plant for you."

There is a warning edge to her reply.

"It's not just a plant, Olly. It's a bloody great bush. And it's not ours to uproot. It's growing through the slats of next door's fence. And, if you remember, you weren't very willing to give me a hand doing anything. You were not even very willing to stir."

She takes advantage of her extrication from the second boot to turn her back on me. And, even as I watch, the inclination of the back of her head tells me the peer in the pot has turned deeply suspicious.

Too late to make it to the door.

"Olly, this dress is *burnt*."

"Only a little."

"A little?" She lifts the dripping garment with her spoon. "Here is a bloody great *hole*."

I can't retreat. It would look obvious.

"Constance, if you ever bothered to try it for yourself, you'd realize that it isn't all that easy to stir with one hand while you're writing with the other."

The look she gives me would have shrivelled Rasputin. The sodden lump of frock drops off the spoon. Dye splashes everywhere.

"Olly, you really are a giant pain up the arse!"

I *hate* it when Constance speaks to me as if we were still married. It's so rude, so presumptuous. Doesn't she realize that, if it weren't for the children, I'd pull the plug on her so fast she'd go spinning down in the economic sewers. She'd know then that, when you're through, you're through. Somehow I can't see the Vegetable King keeping her in the style to which she's accustomed. And, as for earning her own keep, well, ho, ho, ho. She knows as well as I do just how unlikely that scenario is after well-nigh fifteen years of subsidized leisure. She took the greatest care not to slide that one in as a discussion document while she was pushing through the Great Family Readjustment. How long had she been back in her precious house? Three months, was it? Four? I, of course, being the breadwinner, had to keep working till the end of the semester before I could fly home and see my own children. And though I was very kindly accorded my own half of the marital bed, it was quite clear to me, jet-lagged as I was, that some sort of domestic reappraisal had taken place in my absence.

"Whose is this toothbrush? Is it Alasdair Huggett's? Are you actually sleeping with the man now?"

"Oh, lay off, Olly, for God's sake. You're hardly off the bloody plane!"

Hands up all the unmarried people in the back row who don't know what that means. It means: Yes, I am sleeping with Alasdair Huggett, but I would like to have the big row about it later, not now.

She was quite right. I wasn't up to it. I was too tired. My eyes were red-rimmed and my brain was gummy. Up to the very last and into the flight, I'd been struggling with a problem in Analytic Implication. Nor was I in a position to take the quickest tack: total marital outrage. I'd had a small affair of my own. Nothing important, just a little blip. But enough to confuse the discussion. Better to save the whole business till morning. (Constance's morning. It was, of course, already mine.)

Morning (or evening) came. And facts emerged. My estimation of "a little blip" had to be drastically revised in the face of Constance's dramatic response to the few details she managed to squeeze out of me about my brief and unedifying relationship with young Debbie; but over the next few days it became clearer and clearer that my little discontinuity in marital exclusivity was a mere hiccup compared with the cataclysmic earth movements that I found taking place in my own house.

"Who wants to come for a walk?"

"We can't. We're playing with Ally."

The man certainly knew how to dig himself in. I don't think there was a corner of the household he hadn't put his mark on in those few weeks. Even my little wooden chair had been mended. That Ned of his was to be found forever crawling round our floors, shedding wet nappies, and getting tripped over by me and spoiled by Nancy. God knows when Ally ever pushed off home. Ratbag certainly can't have seen anywhere near as much of him as I did.

"Is that man living with us now? Is there some small extension he's knocked up that I don't know about? Have he and his small son moved in for good?"

"Don't be so silly, Olly." But she did look uneasy. And, soon enough, I heard the chew-chew-chewing of the cud up the pipework.

"Constance, I honestly don't think we can go on like this very much longer."

"Oh, Ally. Why on earth not?"

"Well, for one thing I almost can't bear it. I love you and you're still going to bed with him. It isn't fair on me."

Not fair on *him*? Who married the bloody woman in the first place? And what is *fair*?

138

Give Constance her due, she fought back in her ferret-like fashion.

"But he's the children's father. And anyway, I love him and I wouldn't want to hurt him. I don't want to hurt anybody, Ally. It's all very well you thinking that sorting things out will make everything better. But probably it won't. What about Stella? She will be really upset."

"Stella? Upset?"

"She might be."

"Yes, she might, I suppose. And stones might cry."

"Olly would be upset."

"Would he?"

Would I? My pen came to a sudden and distracted halt halfway through the words "interpolation lemma", and if the floorboards hadn't been such creakers, I might have shifted my chair a little closer to the airing cupboard to ensure that I didn't miss further piped enlightenment. As it was, all I did was swing open one of the little wooden doors, and listen harder. Ally, it seems, was laying aside his usual amenable manner. The man was playing for high stakes. My wife.

"I'm not the cheating sort. I can't go on. You'll have to make your mind up. Him or me."

What was she doing? Picking at her nails? I thought I heard the sound of a tiny slap in passing. But nothing else from her. The floor tiles squeaked as Ally the Prosecuting Counsel strode up and down my kitchen in his thick rubber gardening boots, laying our his case. "He has a fine record — for a lodger. No-one is trying to deny him that. He ambles in and our, fetching his tea. His money turns up in the bank account as regular as clockwork, whether he's here or nor. And since he's been back he's stayed our of everyone's hair, and been kind to the children."

The cheek of it! The bloody cheek of it!

"Well, then," said Constance.

That's all she said. That's all there was to it. Was he as exasperated as I was by this pathetic response? There are times when a registered halfwit could produce a more sensible contribution than Constance. But Ally wasn't going to be deterred by her sheer vagueness this time. The man pressed on.

"What's sex with him like now?"

"Fine, thank you," Constance said. (The nearest *she* gets to a loyal wife.)

"Pity," said Alasdair. And then he followed up with what, for him, was unaccustomed clarity:

"The time has come for you to make up your mind. Do you want to be married to a husband or a lodger?"

At this point I was relieved to hear Constance finally pulling herself together sufficiently to go all cunning on our marriage's behalf.

"It all sounds very well and good, Ally. But what about money? We'd be really hard up together, you and I. Neither of us makes beans."

Beans? She earns nothing. Never has.

"If you love me properly, money shouldn't matter."

Get out of that one, Constance. Squirm, squirm, squirm.

"Ally, be sensible. We can't just think of ourselves. There's not just you and me to be considered. There's Nancy and Bonnie, and even Ned most of the time, now

Stella's back at work. There's no need for a big fancy fuss, and divorces and whatnot. Why don't we just take it slowly? Everything's worked out fine so far, apart from you going off in that huff and marrying Stella —"

"You left the country, Constance! You were away six whole years!"

"Well, now I'm back. So why don't we just carry on the way we are? It's only a matter of a few little readjustments. One or two tiny changes . . ."

"You don't want to ask him to leave!"

It's an indictment. I, up the pipes, can tell simply from the ring of his voice that this is the bitterest of indictments. Constance, however, chooses to take it as a bright idea. Women are so bloody slippery.

"Exactly! Why ask him to leave? He needs a home, and we need supporting."

"Constance, this is our lives. We only get one. You're going to have to tell him."

Is she getting rattled?

"I'm going to have to tell him *what*?"

Ally's voice drops. I have to strain to hear.

"Well — sex, for one thing."

"What about sex?" Has she burst into tears? I hear the thud of his great knees as he comes down on them in front of her.

"Constance, you're going to have to talk to him. You're going to have to tell him. Tell him it's over. You are mine. Sex between you two is out."

"Out?"

"Out, out, out. Sex with him is out for you, and he will have to go out for sex."

I waited. I heard nothing. That was it. Her silent acquiescence up the pipes. Our marriage down the drain. And then, out of nowhere suddenly, a horrid little streak of cowardice:

"Need he be told? Can't he just sort of pick it up, gradually?"

Even the Salad Supremo sounded disgusted.

"What? Along with my toothbrush, and my clothes off his hangers?"

A heavy sigh. "You're right. He must be told." And then a brave little rally. "You tell him."

"You have to tell him, Constance. You're his wife."

Not any more, she wasn't. Not from the moment she denied me. When I look back on things, I realize that I have not thought myself bound to Constance in any significant respect since the silence that signalled her utter betrayal. Our marriage finished there. *Finito*. End. There was nothing between us any more but a partly shared past and two partly shared children. And I, for one, felt sufficiently detached to make the next few hours very awkward indeed — swept her affectionately into my arms as I came down the stairs, told her I had been thinking a family holiday might be nice. What did she think of France? — and generally acted my softest self.

It made her nervous, you could tell.

"Olly, whatever you're up to, you have to stop it and we have to talk."

"Talk? I'm a little busy right now, Constance. Talk to Ally instead. You like talking to him."

142

"Oh, Olly, *please!*"

I couldn't keep it up, though. I'm not that mean. In the end I had to lay down my pen and turn to face her. And then, it seemed, she could no longer find the words to get her little newsflash over.

"Constance, your language is guarded to the point of impenetrability. What are you trying to say?"

Tears. More tears. And then back down the stairs to Mission Control.

"I can't tell him. It just won't bloody come out right."

"I'll tell him."

And he did. Strode up the stairs, the Carrot King, and told me where to get off. Once it was out, of course, Constance recovered all her fighting skills. I only had to slide a feeler out to get it bitten, hard.

"What about the children?"

"What *about* the children, Olly?"

"Oh, nothing."

No point in freshening her up for a row, and, for the life of me, I couldn't think of anything they hadn't got used to anyway, over the years. So I didn't bother. And I certainly wasn't going to demean myself by arguing about trivia. Either I accepted the switch-around and shut my mouth, or I put my mind to getting her back sharpish. It wouldn't have been all that difficult. I'm a good man. I'm steady. I am good in bed. She promised to be my wife for ever and ever, and I know her. All that it would have needed was for me to fall on the marital equivalent of Ally's great knees, and beg her to stay, promise her something better, offer her more of myself.

So why on earth didn't I bother to do it?

Because the marriage was over, that's why. How long had we been together? Years and years. We'd gone through all this begging and promising and offering before. It never worked. Most of the time it was my heart that wasn't in it; and once or twice towards the end when I believe I truly did mean well, it turned out her heart was no longer in it either. We simply didn't fit. It didn't work. By the time we split up, she had a grudge against me as huge and pervasive as an inoperable tumour: "You spoil everything for me, Oliver. *Everything*. All the things that I like about the world — looking after babies and children and animals, doing the garden, chatting to people, watching the telly and reading the papers — they're nothing but intrusions and distractions to you. One petty irritation after another keeping you from the only real love of your life: what's in your bloody head. Well, keep your irritation to yourself. Don't come in here and stain the air round me with your impatience and your grumpiness. Piss off with your great black cloud. Stop poisoning *my* life!"

No-one needs much of that. Especially not me. I was as sick of her constant disapproval as she was sick of mine. I was fed up to here with having all my serious desires treated like personality defects. I'm an outsider. I was born and reared that way. I can't pretend to fit in, and I don't even want to. I was as sick of Constance getting on my case as she was sick of me. And the marriage was over.

And all I need is for my former wife to recognize this small but salient fact in our everyday verbal interactions.

*

144

"Pain up the arse yourself, Consrance!"

She turned round from splashing blue dye in the sink, and stared so hard I fen obliged to defend myself.

"You said it first!"

"Oh, shut up, Olly. That was ten minutes ago. You're such a bloody brooder, you drive me mad. If you put a quarter of the care and concern you show for your precious dignity into stirring things properly, you wouldn't have turned Nancy's Brownie uniform into a floorcloth. You're far more of a pain up the arse than me!"

I'm nor forced to respond a second time because she's left the full force of the water from the raps hitting the sodden lump of cloth in the sink, and dye juice is splattering the length of the kitchen.

"Watch out! You're soaking my papers!"

"Oh, sod your bloody papers!"

Not having *that*.

"I can see why Ally's chosen to dally round at Ratbag's. She's probably a lot pleasanter company than you are."

"Don't you believe it." She's really pummelling away in the sink now. "Fetching poor Ned these days is a real operation. Ally probably hasn't got within a grenade's throw of the house yet"

Does Constance have a sixth sense? Why did she turn round then, to glance at me?

"Olly! Don't eat those berries! Spit them out at *once*!"

I felt quite shaken, looking at the half-chewed purple pulp.

"That's your fault, Constance. You should never have left them there!"

She swept up the punnet and hurled it in the bin. "Oh, Oliver! Sometimes I think you're not all there, honestly."

"I wasn't thinking."

"You're always thinking. That's your problem. You think too much. All the blood in your brain rushes to the really clever bits and there's none left over to warm up the roots."

Introduction to Advanced Neuro-Physiology by Constance Rosen. Sighing, I tipped what was left of my handful of berries into the rubbish bin, after the rest, and started to wipe the stain on my palms off on the frilly apron. She flew across the room, screeching "No, Olly! No!" Could I do nothing right? Raising my arms above my head in surrender, I came very close to scowling at Constance as she unceremoniously pushed me round to unknot her precious pinny. But she had saved my life — well, saved me from several hours sitting shivering on a cold lavatory, thinking of death. I could at least try to say something comforting and friendly.

"I expect they'll be here any minute, happy as sandboys."

She snorted.

"I doubt it. Ned usually arrives in floods of tears, and Ally takes hours to calm down after tangling with Ratbag."

This is divorce for you, of course. You hear about this sort of thing all the time.

"What is it with this business of Ned coming over here? This Stella Ratbag must be half-unhinged. You'd think she would be only too pleased to have a day off

146

child-rearing every now and again. It's not as if Ally's incapable. That was quite masterly, last night, the way he coped with Nancy and that baby pigeon. Killing small animals off is no party. Remember when I had to drown that crippled mouse? I thought that Ally was a real professional. I even quite enjoyed the little funeral. What is this woman's problem, for heaven's sake?"

"How the hell should I know?"

Usually, I make a point of taking very little interest in the other half of Constance's life. You'd think she'd be more appreciative when I do make the effort.

"You've met her, haven't you?"

"Once or twice, very briefly."

"Is she attractive?"

"Yes."

"More than you?"

If that Brownie frock she's wringing was a chicken, it would be dead by now.

"I can't judge, can I?"

Really, this sort of prudish pussyfooting round plain facts does annoy me.

"Don't be so silly, Constance. Of course you can judge. If you and she were in a jumble sale, who would people buy first? You or her?"

"Her, I expect."

She is attractive, then. Very attractive.

"So what went wrong between this luscious beauty and the Parsnip Prince?"

"Nothing went wrong, Oliver. Ally just realized how horrible she was."

"And how long did that take?"

"Five weeks."

I didn't think I could have heard her right.

"Five *weeks*?"

Constance was striding out of the back door towards the clothes line, leaving a trail of blue drips. "Five weeks is nothing," I said, pursuing her. "Five weeks is a mere blink."

She was still hard to hear through a mouthful of pegs, but I did think I caught:

"Not if you're single, it isn't."

Constance is right. Time's different for the unmarried. If someone as soppy as Ally was lonely and yearning, I should think five weeks was more than enough time to fall in love and rush off and get hitched. It would leave plenty of time in hand to come to the grim realization that he had blown it, and it was all a terrible mistake.

"Only five weeks, though! Why didn't he cut out at once?"

"Stella was pregnant, of course."

"Why didn't she have an abortion? Is she Catholic?"

"No. Spiteful."

Constance responded to my blank expression with one of her little probably-not-worth-rattling-his-bars looks before she bothered to explain.

"Spiteful because it meant he had to stay."

Of course. Staying together because of the children. It's not a concept that has loomed over-large in my particular world view up till now, perhaps because Constance devoted so much of our own married life to pointing out my flaws as a parent and partner. Personally, I was led rather to believe it would be very much to everyone's advantage if I were to disappear in a sudden puff of smoke. But I do recognize that, in the general run of things, it is a powerful doorstop against that one, last, cataclysmic slam.

"But then, when you came back for good —?"

Constance spat pegs, and glared.

"That's right. Blame me! Everyone else does. Why not you? After I came back, Ally just walked out!"

Hear that? He just walked out. Constance disturbed my work for weeks with her agonizing and her public guilt. Ally just walked out. There's a man for you. A tribute to his Scottish schooling. The man just upped and off — possibly the one thing he's ever had in common with Bertrand Russell (except for the fact that, according to Constance — who, of course, brings the deep perceptions of her own *Weltanschauung* to her skip-reading of the great three-volumed autobiography — Ally and he share exactly the same star sign). They both just got on bikes and pedalled off.

So did my mother once, apparently. I know because Solly told me. Joe told him. For years Joe was the only one who knew. It seems he watched her hauling the old bike out of the garden shed, scraping the pedals against her legs and seeming not even to notice, let alone care. And that's what panicked him.

"Where are you going?" he asked her, running up. "Can I come?" She turned. And he says that when he saw the expression on her face, he suddenly found himself changing the question.

"*Why* are you going?"

"Why should I stay? You give me one good reason, and I'll stay."

That's what she said. He swore that was exactly what she said. Solly did push — it was years ago, he must have forgotten the details — but under cross-examination Joe stayed firm. That's what she said to him. That's all she said. In telling me, and ever afterwards, Sol took the hard view. What sort of mother was she, for heaven's sake, that she could leave that challenge hanging in the air, and pedal off down the street? How could she leave one of her own (not even one of his) so robbed of confidence and self-esteem that every failure after that, each shrivelling friendship, every fitful job, would end up seeming like a natural progression from his shy and tongue-tied inability to thump his birdy little chest and yell in her face. "Me! I'm a very good reason! Me! Me! *Me*!"

We all lost out from that one. Look at Sol. He could swim, couldn't he? *Surely* he could swim. And look at me. I am light years beyond my childhood, and, thanks to Constance, I am well aware that children can reduce strong women to pulp. But I still feel quite wretched when I think back, and have to face the fact that, if my brother didn't count enough to keep Mum from getting on that bike of hers, neither of course did I. And what gets to me most is no-one gained. What is it with these women? Ally and Bertrand Russell at least won their freedom. My mother was back home well before dark. (Nowhere to go? No-one to take her in?) I didn't register she'd even left. But when I think about my brother's peculiar disappearance, and wonder whether he actually

150

took his own life or just somehow otherwise altered himself out of existence, I can't help wondering what difference those hours made. Oddly enough, I sometimes think I might have a trace memory of noticing him hanging about, kicking the heads off the weeds round the back gate that day. Did he look strange? There must be something in your face others can read the afternoon your mother (or your wife of fifteen years) tells you that, after all, you count for shit.

"Who counts for shit?"

Oh, Christ. How much popped out this time? Preserve me, dear gods, from Constance's lecture of the character-warping nature of male self-pity (free Personality Dangers Courtesy Factsheet No 42) available for delivery any time, any place, by post or telephone, or at the top of her voice across the kitchen table. Lucky for me my desperate, hunted stare over the washing-line yields one small chance of escape.

"I said it looks like Ally's feelings must count for shit. He's back. But Ned's not with him."

Pegs fly like rain as Constance hares across the garden towards her shambling and defeated hero.

Phew.

Back to work at last.

CHAPTER
SEVEN

Excuse me. This is your Constance speaking. Pardon me trespassing in this pillowcase for a moment, but I have a Public Service Announcement for all of Olly's readers. It is this: "Don't be the one to ask for the divorce."

I mean it. It's not worth it. You think, all you lot trembling on the brink, that your spouse is going to throw a monumental wobbly, grumble a little bit whilst coming to terms, and then fold neatly up and disappear, so things will be all right. Well, you are wrong. The one who cuts the knot just cannot win. It is a rule. Be warned, all shallow paddlers everywhere, the water's cold out here. Stay where you are. Enjoy yourselves. Make the most of your casual little affairs, your secret passions and your odd nights off. But don't try wading out this far, you'll only be sorry. There's more lurking in these deep waters than you think. Come out no further than waist high, and I mean it. You take my word for it. Stay in your depth!

Not that I'm claiming staying married does you any good. Just look at Olly's mum. Got on her bike and rode away (probably the first hour the woman had been left in peace since she was last in labour). Came back, served almost all her term, and then gets blamed for Solly's death, Joe's disappearance, Olly's temperament. What do the buggers want? Do they want *blood*?

Yes, probably. And half the time, to watch them scowling around the house, snarling at the pets and the children, you'd think they wanted a divorce as well. But, take my advice, leave that particular messy household chore to them. However bad things get, don't be the one to suggest the short separation "just to take stock". Ignore all the warning expressions — "bit of an emotional rut", "some time to find myself", "only one life". Don't say the D-word. Just for this once, let the sods do their own bloody dirty work. For, I tell you, it is a fearsome thing to spend your life trying to be a kind person and a good parent and then, after all your efforts, see yourself end up with absolutely everything: the house, the kids, and *all*, all the blame.

Take Christmas, for example. The hell of that can start the moment Alasdair puts down the phone and says (rather unnecessarily, I always think, since he knows I've been listening to every word):

"He's coming."

"He said he wasn't!"

"But he is."

"When?"

"Thursday, he said. Some time during the day. He's not sure when."

"Is he going to need a lift in from the airport?"

I'm not going to get an answer, that's quite clear. Ally's already turned his back to stare out of the kitchen window, his fists bunched at his sides. I don't need any answer anyway. I know what Oliver's arrangements are like. First he'll need to go all the way over to one side of the town to find the one person who knows the address of the flat that he's borrowed. Then all the way over to the other to pick up the key. Then back to the first side again to put the key in the keyhole.

"He'll take up the whole of Thursday."

"Constance, Thursday is Christmas Eve!"

I'm muttering already. One phone call and I'm muttering. "He does it to torture us. He must do. He's like that ghastly old advertisement for Prudential Pensions. "I really ought to book a flight", "I must book a flight", "Oh, how I wish I'd bothered to book a flight!", "Unless there's a sudden cancellation, I simply don't know what I'm going to do!" We make more and more arrangements that don't include him — and then this! He does the one thing you would never think. He travels on a day when no-one in his right mind would cross the world!"

"Easy," warns Alasdair. "Ears on stalks . . ."

But I'm not listening, of course. I'm worrying about Oliver.

"He's going to ruin Christmas, I see it coming. He'll be all grumpy with jet-lag. The children will worry themselves sick that he's alone with nothing to eat but sliced bread and long-life milk. They can't spend Christmas Day with him. They *can't*. He'll have no presents, no decoration, no tree, no food! And wherever he's staying he won't be able to get the heating to work. It'll be dank and nasty and stone-cold. It's far too late to ask anyone else to invite him. He'll simply have to come to us."

"No, Constance! No!"

I spread my hands.

"Ally, we have no choice."

"I do," says Alasdair. "If Oliver comes here for Christmas again, I'm leaving."

"Be sensible," I said. "Think of the children."

It is a nightmare, this business. Are you getting the message? Don't even bother to think of leaving your spouse unless the person you plan on fetching up with second time around happens to be a saint, thrilled beyond measure to take on board your jittery, weeping-in-the-night, up-rooted self, your tense, resentful children and their food prejudices, your children's smelly gerbils, your rancid cat, and constant, constant inroads from your ex-spouse.

No-one is perfect . . .

"If Oliver comes here again, I'm leaving."

"Be sensible. Think of the children."

"You think of them," snapped Ally. "They're right behind you."

And so they were, of course. With ears on stalks.

"Is Dad on his way home?"

"Daddy!"

(Daddy. The very word is like a bell, to toll you back . . .)

"Is Dad really coming? I thought you told us all the flights were full."

"And so they are, till Thursday."

"Thursday? Thursday is Christmas Eve!"

I am ignoring the silence that has begun to emanate, quite palpably, from Alasdair.

"Yes," I say brightly. "Isn't that nice?"

Suspicious Bonnie remains unconvinced.

"But where's he going to stay?"

Now everyone is looking towards him expectantly, Ally feels forced to respond.

"He said friends of someone he teaches are renting him their flat."

"The friends of someone he teaches? *Students*?"

"He didn't say."

"I bet they are!" cried Bonnie. "They must be. No-one except for students would still be renting out their flat two days before Christmas!" A worse thought struck. "Or maybe no-one else will take the place. Maybe it's going to be as bad as that one last year, all freezing and slimy and disgusting, with woodlice crawling in the kitchen cabinets, and silverfish slithering about in the greasy old bath!"

Now Nancy's face is crumpling.

"He did promise he'd never, ever rent anything as horrible as that again," I have to remind my stricken children.

"He promised that the time before, too," Alasdair spitefully reminds me in turn. "Have you forgotten? The time he ended up in that nasty little place under the bypass."

"I never saw that one," said Bonnie.

"Neither did I."

No, no, my sweet, protected babes. You never saw that one. Your mother rated it PG at a glance, and never let

156

you go. Even your father only held out in it four days. But, thank you, Ally. No, I have not forgotten it. Naturally it's not a question one strides up and down the streets of one's home town asking, but wouldn't you think most people probably end up remembering not just the first time that they went to bed with someone, but also the last? And the last time I ever went to bed with Oliver was in that nasty little place under the bypass. Sixteen years, we were married. Sixteen years! We must have done it a lot. We probably did it every day at least for the first couple of years. And then about every other day at least for the next ten years or so. And probably still about every third day, for one reason or another, towards the end. So, with the help of Bonnie's regulation school multi-function calculator, I calculate that, if the battery's not flat, we must have done it at least three thousand and forty-one times. At least. And yet already, under the pressure of a different body, the memory of all those times with Oliver is getting a bit impacted, squashing into a sort of amiable blur about the way he looked and felt and made me feel. Just my bad luck, then, that our first time was in a ditch, and the last in the very nastiest rented property that I have ever seen.

Even staunch Oliver was dismayed. Though for the entire length of our marriage I'd thought he'd shown a disconcertingly high tolerance for grime and disorder, it seemed he too could recognize the difference between a last tenant's sloppy exit and sheer ineradicable filth.

He dropped his suitcase on the cracking lino, and looked quite wretched.

"I can't stay here."

(If Oliver says it, believe me, it must be true. He doesn't speak for effect. He doesn't know how.)

I drew my skirt back from an encrusted table leg, and leaned towards the one tiny window. All that was visible through its streaked panes was the drab grey of some vast concrete strut. The flat was shuddering horribly underfoot, and the sound of the traffic on the bypass was deafening.

"I simply can't understand it. He sounded such a nice man on the phone . . ."

"Is that a tidemark, do you think, round the walls?"

"'Practically out in the country,' he said."

The lorries thundered overhead. I had a sudden vision of their giant wheels running over my Nancy and squashing her flat.

"Those lorries must have thirty wheels apiece . . ."

"This is disgusting. This is *snot*. Dried *snot*."

"You'll have to come back to the house."

Oliver, I remember, paused only long enough to make me feel really uncomfortable before he answered:

"With him there? No, I don't think so, Constance, thank you very much."

How quickly sympathy catapults into resentment. I'm sick of feeling guilty about Oliver. Let him turn to me with his skin grey from a night sky-high, his face sagging with exhaustion and disappointment. All he'll find is that I will savage him.

"It's your own fault! You should have let me find you a decent place. It's stupid looking from eight thousand miles away."

"Oh, shut up, Constance! Can't you get it in your thick head that, in the circumstances, I don't want your help?"

It's things like that "in the circumstances" that make me want to take a meat-axe to him.

"Olly, it never occurs to you, does it, that you're not the only person in the world to have feelings? What about the children? What about Alasdair and me? How do you think it's going to go for us when Bonnie and Nancy see us in the house and you in this dump?"

"Fuck you and bloody Alasdair!"

"Well, fuck you, too!"

And in the end, of course, I did, because that's how quarrels between the two of us always fetched up — in bed in tears, in tears in bed. We spread Oliver's raincoat over this one because I really didn't like the look of it. And all I remember about our three thousand and forty-second, and last, time together was that I was taking great care not to stretch out too far in any direction and brush the stained walls or the sticky bedhead. It didn't take too long. And for all we were still married to one another that year, it still felt like adultery — as if Alasdair, watching the children the other side of town, might suddenly sense just what it was delaying my return, leap on his bike and pedal like a madman along the bypass to spot us at it through the filthy window panes.

After, tucking and buttoning, I said to Oliver:

"You won't tell, will you? Nobody. Ever. You do promise?"

In search of his sock, he spoke to whatever horrors lay under the bed.

"What? Risk your nice new Ally's peace of mind? Good Lord, no."

See? Twist off your ring and fling it out. But who else will you ever know so deeply, so well, that you can tell even before you speak which of your little slights and insensitivities will be taken up and picked at for hours on end, and which, like mine that day, will be passed over with companionable generosity, on the small stepping-stone of an Ally-baiting chuckle:

"Quite sure he'd do the same for me — probably has!"

No. Shan't forget that place.

"I never saw that one."

"Neither did I."

"Well, you were lucky. And I expect that he's found somewhere really nice this time."

"I hope it's near the shops. The last time he found somewhere really nice, it was about a thousand miles from the shops, and he made me and Bonnie carry all the shopping."

"Nancy, he made you carry one plastic bag containing two boxes of man-sized paper tissues and one roll of tinfoil. And Bonnie was given one jumbo pack of lavatory rolls and one carton of plastic drinking straws. He himself carried absolutely everything else. I heard your father's side of the story several times after the quarrel, and I believe him."

"He does lie, though. He lied to us. He told us we were just popping in there for one or two things."

"One or two little things to keep him going, he said."

"We were there practically all day!"

"I had to be put in the trolley and pushed, I got so tired."

"Up and down every single aisle."

"Reading all the labels."

"Checking them off against his list of E numbers."

"He does it because he loves you," I told them. "He does it because he cares about your health."

Ally's no help.

"It used to drive you mad enough," he says. "After a shopping session with him, you used to come back half-mental."

Well, there's another problem right there, though few but me would dare come out with it in these dark times of positive thinking about the children's relationship with the ex-spouse. Why should you expect the poor little mites to put up with all the dreadful habits you couldn't stand? If she was a vile-tempered, domineering harpy, why shouldn't they get a bit of open sympathy for having to stick it out all week and every other weekend? Take *you* back and you probably couldn't even hack it civilly through the small gap between a late supper and the start of "Newsnight". And what about him? If he drinks and slobbers and burps, and patronizes everybody in earshot, why should your children be expected to cringe their way through half their weekends and their holidays without a bit of moral support from you? I know what experts say. I've read the books. A child's supposed to be all the better for a strong and continuing relationship with the absent parent. Well, fair enough. I suppose we shall have to accept that. (Not got much choice.) But while this fashion for not bad-mouthing lasts, let's not forget the marriage didn't crack for nothing. You were getting away from *something*, weren't you? And just because *you* managed to get out, there's no reason to forget how it was.

"It was awful. Awful! I swear to God that sometimes I'd as soon have planted an ice pick between his eyes as push the trolley round another corner! I can't think how I stood it as long as I did. Shopping with Oliver is a day trip to *hell*." (It's not my fault. Ally should never have started me off. Everyone has an infallible launch pad into the horrors of their last relationship, and mention of Olly's shopping habits is mine.) "I'll tell you Oliver's trouble. He can't 'just' do anything at all. If Oliver ever says 'just', then beware. 'I'll just be a minute' means he'll be gone for hours. 'I'll just have a quick word with the neighbours about their dustbins.' *Years* of resentment smouldering both sides of the fence. You can't even pull out their bloody deadly nightshade! But, as for shopping! 'I'll just nip in here and pick up one or two things.' Before you know where you are, you're beached for the whole day! Fetched up on aisle No 4 while Oliver tries to remember whether E 463 is hydroxypropylwhatsit or just fatty acid, and whether a 950-gramme box of liver-flavoured Munchies will work out at more or less of a bargain than a fifteen-ounce can of end-of-range Chompy."

Ally was trying to warn me, but I wasn't watching.

"Oh, shut up!" (Bonnie — my own, loyal Bonnie — turning on me for all the world as if I were Oliver!) "For

God's sake, lay off. Leave him alone! He isn't even here yet, and you're picking on him!"

Scowling quite horribly, she grabs her sister's hand and pulls the quietly weeping Nancy after her, out of the room.

"That wasn't very sensible, was it?"
"Oh, shut up, Ally. Just shut up!"

I'll tell you what I want to know. I want to know exactly what it *is* about Oliver that begets so much havoc. Look at us. He isn't even on the bloody plane, and we're all carping at one another, nerves in shreds. How can one human being, eight thousand miles away, have such a devastating effect? Is he, perhaps, not really human at all, but some pitiless divinity made flesh? He has the strength of twenty, for a start. He is unstoppable and he is dauntless. His travelling schedule alone would fell a normal person within days. For Oliver, crossing the globe means nothing. *Nothing*. A lecture here, a conference there, visiting a department somewhere else, a quick detour on the way back for a peep at the children, and then kick to his swish university to hand in another pile of papers to the typists, and start all over again. Chart him across the world map in the kitchen with little lines of coloured wool, and in no time at all you'd have a tangle that would take weeks to unravel. He takes so many planes, he's reached the stage of complaining about the food and the service. If you want to know what I think, I think that's dangerous. Like many another earthbound, I think the only sane behaviour towards planes is staying out of them. Or, if push really comes to shove, sitting there, desperately willing the thing to stay up.

"I certainly hope he isn't flying with that cut-price airline again . . ."

Ally, still stung, is not above deliberate misunderstanding.

"I'm not surprised. How long were you waiting for him at the airport that time? Was it six hours? Seven?"

"Only on the first day. Be fair."

"Oh, that's right. On the second they told you as soon as you got to the front of the queue that he had quite definitely been re-routed to Frankfurt."

Since I refused to rise, he jerked the bait.

"And that's when both the kids burst into tears."

"Oh, what a memory you have, Ally!"

Slamming the door behind me, I rushed out. I sometimes think, between the three of us, there's nothing we all remember exactly the same. Oliver was pontificating all through supper last night. (All poor Ally did was ask why the autobiography was taking so long, and Olly was down his throat.) "What is the point of writing anything if you don't get it absolutely right? If it's not true and full, then it's worth nothing. Those are the principles on which I've done thirty years of philosophical thinking, and I couldn't abandon them now if I tried." He took the opportunity to have a little sideways swipe at me, of course. "That's why I'm here, no doubt. So Constance can peel the skin off till it hurts, and I end up writing an account of things so truthful even she can't carp at it any longer!"

164

But Olly's truth isn't mine. And mine isn't Ally's. We all lead separate lives. Alasdair tries to bait me with the memory of one whole Christmas Eve spent being misinformed about the movements of Flight PK 206, but what he doesn't know and I'd never tell is that I was happy hanging around that airport, waiting for Oliver. I'd never missed anyone in the world as badly as I missed Olly those first few months, and I will tell you one thing from the heart, I never intend to miss anyone like that again. Not anyone. Not ever. It was all right for him. After the first bout of fury and distress, he flew off on great flapping wings of outrage and came conveniently to land amongst his huge research grants, his conference deadlines, and hosts of sympathetic colleagues. Me? I got the haunted house. I'm serious. Week after week, nothing inside my head, however small, however silly, could come to rest because he wasn't there. It was a mystery. I could hardly believe it. It wasn't, for heaven's sake, as if Olly had ever taken much interest in anything I told him. He never actually seemed to be paying attention. If I was called away in the middle of some riveting tale about what had happened to me down at the shops, he never ambled after me to hear the rest. And if, by some miracle, he did happen to catch the whole story, he wouldn't remember a word of it five minutes later. And yet . . . and yet . . . the coal delivered sodden wet again, a joke from Bonnie, snatches of neighbours' quarrels overheard — the phantoms drifted round my head for days on end for want of the customary domestic exorcism: telling Olly.

Why wouldn't Ally do? I don't know why. Perhaps for the same reason Stringbean wouldn't do if Nancy got run over: not the same. When Olly left, a whole chunk of my life went down the drain, along with the do-you-remembers of a dozen years and a whole way of talking. I felt bereft, like the last member of some aboriginal tribe who lifts his eyes from the body of his dying friend to realize his whole world's gone. There's no-one left to understand him. I could say, "It was as mouldy as that cheese we bought in Gloucester," and instantly Olly would be apprised of the full perfidy of the grocer. "Their house is just like the Furleys'." He knew to shudder. "I felt as giddy as I did that time you bullied me up the bell tower. Worse!"

Who speaks this language now? No-one. It was our own. I want to write to Olly all the time, for fear that if our private language disappears, the part of me that speaks it will shrivel up and leave me nothing but a hollow place and sixteen wasted years. I understand now why the bereaved write letters to their dead, why widows used to sit in circles tapping table tops, why those who've lost their partner let Death in. He makes a little foothold, don't you see? Uses the space left when your old private language is wiped out, and if you don't fill the gap, quick, with other things, he'll take the chance to grow. Cancer, pneumonia — he doesn't care. Like all the displaced and the dispossessed, you have to learn another language fast, or you're a goner. Take people. I had to learn how to describe them all over again. "He has frizzy red hair." "She was wearing an ancient flowery tea-gown." How does Oliver manage now that I'm not around to understand exactly what he means when he says "a beard like McFie's" or "hair the same colour as that man in Hove who caught me kicking his cat". I'm lost now I can't say "It was a dress just like that tent thing that my mother wore when she had shingles." I dread to think what the police would do if I were ever witness to some crime. The poor sods would never get an adequate description out. They'd have to rope in half my friends and dozens of my past acquaintances just to make a start on the artist's impression. "Eyes like that lifeguard at the Oakeshott pool — no, not the one who does Thursdays, the other one. Ears like that lollipop man I never trusted, the one who got six months. And, oh yes, the villain wore a shirt just like that one I bought at the Harrods sale and Oliver claims he "lost" at the Fourth Leamington Conference."

Pathetic. And that is, frankly, how I felt. Honestly, I look back now and I think I must have assumed that, when we split up, the image of Oliver would vanish slowly but surely from my psyche like the Cheshire Cat, leaving only the scowl. Well, ho, ho, ho.

It serves me right, of course. I should have thought. You don't marry someone like Oliver and get out unscathed. You're bound to find, as soon as you gingerly inspect yourself after, that you're still covered in marks. To this day, for example, I can't keep a large sum of money in a current account, it would never occur to me to cook anything with coconut, and I couldn't buy a blender without reading *Which*? first. I simply can't stand Scarlatti, whom Olly played night and day the week Nancy coughed her lungs up from whooping cough. I'd never try and drown a crippled mouse — rather stamp on its head, frankly, after what I saw.

Ally's scarred too. His time with Ratbag didn't do him any good. He won't go into shops (except for food), still wakes up sometimes lying like a ramrod on the far side of the bed, and has an absolute horror of Weston-super-Mare, where they spent four days in a caravan. What about Oliver? What has he carried off from all those years (apart from most of our trunks and suitcases, and all of the nice set of leather overnight bags)? A sense, I'm sure, that he will never again allow himself to become even mildly fond of anyone, however attractive, who doesn't like him just the way he is. "You'll never change!" I yelled at him one day. He looked at me so coldly. "Constance, if you weren't who you are, I wouldn't have to, would I?" And that was that.

I ask you though, was it my fault? When I met Oliver I was nineteen. I had been changing for years — up a bit, out a bit, you name it, I changed it. I had been changing practically all the time since I was one day old. How was I supposed to know that the party was over? *Now* I know people don't alter, except for a little around the edges, once they are grown. But I didn't know that then. Neither did he. We got on horribly from the day we met, but both of us thought things could change for the better. I thought I'd change him. He thought he'd change me.

Well, fuck that for a lark. Why didn't anyone tell us? I was in full-time education fifteen years. I learned all sorts of things I've never needed since. But the one thing they could have taught me that might have made a

168

difference to my life is that the only good test of whether a marriage is going to last is whether the two of you get on from the start. Did you know that? Probably not. You're probably still worrying about all those other old things they were forever warning people about: difference in age, race, class, religion. Problems with money and sex. But it turns out that none of these things is important. Honestly. When it comes to the crunch of choosing a partner, nothing is as important as whether, in the first months you had one another seriously in mind, the two of you chummed along amiably to granny's party or round the shops, down the allotment or up the Odeon. Be warned. If you fetched up, even only once or twice, snarling at one another over the spice racks in the delicatessen, or having a heated discussion behind his mother's garage doors, or even just sulking quietly in between phone calls, you may as well not have bothered. The marriage is *doomed*.

Why isn't anyone told? Why aren't engagements compulsory? Why don't your family and friends have to submit signed affidavits on your behalf? Everyone frets about the breakdown of family life, with parents drinking themselves silly and children getting bashed up. Most of the loony-bins are bursting at the seams, and practically every marriage you know ends up in disaster. Yet here's this one simple fact no school-leaver ever knows because the morons who arrange the syllabus are so busy stuffing your schooldays with things like capillary action in plants and long division they never even think to mention it. They ought to be going around putting up posters!

I feel quite bitter. I could have got along without long division. In fact, I have. As for capillary action — for heaven's sake! There are instructions on my house-plant labels and, anyway, I'm not an idiot. Left to myself I would have cracked the system in the end. The worst that could have happened in the meantime is that I might have lost a couple of cinerarias or a gloxinia.

But not knowing how to choose the right husband first time around has almost done for me. And countless others. Because, after all, it is as often as not the very thing that makes two people so utterly wretched together that attracts the poor buggers to one another in the first place. It was Oliver's sheer gloominess that appealed to me. I saw it as a challenge! I didn't know that people couldn't change. I was convinced that I could make him *happy*. And it's a good job that Oliver's not the altruistic sort, or I might be suspicious on his behalf, wondering why my dizzy personality appealed to him. At least I can be pretty sure the same diseased notion wasn't swimming round his head while he was eyeing me. "Oh, goody! An opportunity to teach a flighty girl, (a), how to be reasonable, and, (b) a useful corollary — how to *think*."

I got the crummier end of the bargain. It might be hard cheese to end up with me, but it's a truly terrible thing to love the very quality in a man that makes him so sombre and inflexible that you can't live with him. Watch Olly shave, for example. He stands perfectly still. He barely moves from start to finish. There's none of that fancy head-cocking and soapy jaw-fingering you see in other men, or on the telly. My Oliver stares ahead, into the brown of his own eyes, just like a private in a firing squad who knows it could easily be himself ten yards out there in front, strapped to the post. He works from left to right, from up to down; and you can't winkle a word out of him from that first steady screwing of the new blade into the razor to the last slap of Mickey Mouse flannel around his ears. He looks so grave. I've learned a lot since Olly left. I've learned that, just as there is a curse on people who marry without love, there's hell in store for those who part without hatred. I'm warning you, don't risk it. It doesn't work. All that will happen is that you, like me, will find yourself perched on the airport railings year after year, waiting for someone who is *implacable*.

"I'll sit in the back, I think. With the children."

"Suit yourself, Olly. What a pity I didn't think to bring a peaked cap."

Unholy advent. We are off again. It goes from bad to worse, with Ally cheated yet again out of his turn with Ned ("The bitch! I show up exactly at seven, as arranged, and no-one's there. The house is dark! No note. Nothing!"), the children squabbling over the free airline slippers, and Olly unwilling to pick up his bags and push off to his cold and unseen flat.

"Olly, it's after midnight. Either you'll have to sleep here, or you must go."

"There's no point in my going now, Constance. I wouldn't sleep. It's only tea-time for me."

"But I can't stay awake any longer. We had to get the food shopping done really early, so I could have the car to come and pick you up. If you want a lift to Kent Place, you'll have to go now."

"Why don't I stay here and play the piano for a bit, then get a taxi?"

"A taxi? On Christmas Eve?"

"Ally will take me, then. You'll drive me to Kent Place, won't you, Ally?"

"I'd be delighted, Oliver."

"Ally can't drive you, Oliver. Ally's drunk. I'm the one taking you home, and I'm tired."

"Oh, come on, Constance. Relax. Have another drink. You can always sleep late in the morning."

"I can't have another drink, Oliver. I'm driving you home. And I can't sleep late in the morning. I think you must have forgotten what things are like round here. How am I supposed to sleep late with Nancy charging around the house, shrieking about what she found in her stocking?"

"Stockings! Of course! I've brought the perfect gift! Now where did I put it? In the big suitcase or the little one?"

"Oh, Olly, please. Don't start unpacking!"

"I'm not unpacking, Constance. See? I'm simply lifting one or two little items out of my suitcase temporarily and laying them neatly on the carpet, so I can get at this present."

"Can't it wait?"

"It's Christmas Eve, isn't it? You're giving Bonnie and Nancy those stockings. Why can't I put something in?"

"Because they're full."

"They can't be that full. You can squeeze this in. Take something of your own out, to make room."

"Olly, it's half-past twelve! Can't you leave it, for God's sake?"

"Leave it?" He looks up from his enchanted circle of spread books and papers, shirts and underwear. "Why should I leave it? Too inconvenient, is it, Constance, for me to give a present to my own daughter?"

The old black magic. And, of course, it works.

"Oh, all right. If I take out the Magic Bubbles and these chocolate coins, will that give you enough room?"

"No, I think this will have to come out as well."

There is a pause, while Oliver looks at the growing heap of spilled presents and has a think, and I hope he isn't going to think about wrapping.

"Is there some Christmas paper, Constance?"

"Sorry. All gone."

"You must have something in the house. I don't mind if it's crumpled."

Ally's eyes warn me, over his fourth stiff drink within the hour, not to go looking for paper for Oliver at quarter to one in the morning. But where's the choice? Oliver knows me like he knows his own right hand. He knows I hoard wrapping-paper. We were *married*.

"Where is it, Constance? You tell me, and I'll get it."

It's in the cupboard outside the bedroom, of course — our old bedroom.

"That's all right. I'll get it."

I'm on my feet, but so is Alasdair. Rooting through all the spillage from his suitcases, Oliver pretends not to hear Ally's carefully measured goodnight, or notice when he follows me out of the room, taking my arm.

"I'm away to bed now. Are you coming?"

I keep my voice down. "You go on. I'll be along in a bit."

"You've been up since six, don't forget. And we've a long day ahead of us tomorrow."

"I'm coming, Ally. I won't be a moment."

Ally pursues me over to the cupboard where, quite distracted, I am rummaging through my hoard.

"He may be on California time, but Nancy isn't. I'd come along to bed if I were you."

"In a minute, Ally. Let me just take him this."

"And then you'll be back? Straight away?"

"As soon as I can."

"Constance —"

I shake him off. "Ally, for heaven's sake! I'm a grown-up! I can decide my own bedtime!"

The bedroom door won't slam. Praise be to Scottish Schools, the door won't slam. But I will hear it click.

Click!

One down. And one to go. When I come back into the sitting room, I find that Oliver has tipped Nancy's Magic Bubbles pot out of its wrapping, and is trying to slide his own gift inside the crumpled paper shell.

"I'm not sure this is going to fit after all."

"Oh, Oliver! You should have been more patient!"

"Sorry. I didn't know if you'd be coming back."

"Why shouldn't I come back? I said I would."

He shrugs.

"Well, you know . . . One o'clock. Bedtime, and all that."

Is he unhinged? Could he do that to me? Go off and sleep with a new wife in our old bed, and leave me

174

kneeling there on Christmas Eve amid the chaos of my suitcases, and one small, unwrapped gift? Or is he torturing me to pass the time?

I have claws too.

"How's Debbie?"

"Debbie? I don't see Debbie any more."

"The children did mention someone named Karen . . ."

"Karen? She's just a friend."

"And Marie-Claire?"

"Marie-Claire? Oh, Marie-Hélène."

"Marie-Hélène, then."

Olly looks up at last.

"Is this the Spanish Inquisition, Constance? May I take a turn? How are things between you and Alasdair?"

"Everything's going well enough."

"What's sex with him like?"

"Fine, thank you."

"Good as with me, then. That must be an improvement. I can remember you complaining the fellow was so shy he used to try and get away with taking cuttings."

"No, no. Times change. He's definitely into cross-pollination now."

"You'll want to be off to bed, then, won't you? What with it being so late . . ."

I sit and watch him struggle with the sticky-tape. The paper, I notice suddenly, is swarming with smug little Easter bunnies in tartan trews wheeling heaps of bright eggs round in barrows. But Oliver hasn't noticed, and I don't give a shit. I'm thinking. I am thinking: Is this *it*? Is this life after divorce? Have we begun the long slow slide into emotional dishonesty that makes mutual friends avoid divorcing couples like the plague? I pretend Debbie (or Karen, or Marie-Hélène) makes up for home and kids and everything he lost. In return Olly can tell himself that, if I chose Ally and home over him and exile, I must be quite indifferent to him, and can drift off to bed without a second thought. I see why everyone does it. It's terribly tempting. If you can make out your ex-partner's actually sitting rather pretty, you feel your conscience lighten. And maybe this way things even work out better. Perhaps the only sensible thing in the long run is to ignore the fact that what you're telling yourself is no more than the same dishonest crap you've heard dished up by others down the years, and thoroughly despised: "There was no need for her to be so strapped for cash. Thousands of women with children as young as ours manage to work full-time." "He could have seen them over the holidays. It wasn't my fault that the only fortnight he could get off work was the two weeks my parents took them down to Cornwall."

Sooner the better, perhaps. Get it all over. The last few good intentions can boil up, fuelled by your self-deception or by his. At least this way you know exactly where you stand. You hate him. He hates you. Without this prop, you'll probably end up like Stringbean's pretty Aunty Sue, whose feelings were so torn through her divorce that when she walked past George's car in town and saw the parking meter on the cusp, she burst into tears of frustration and rage, unable to decide whether to feed ten pence in the slot and save him, or let the fucker get clamped. Poor thing fetched up in such a dreadful state it took two traffic wardens to drag her off. She was kicking the meter so ferociously she bent it.

She's better now, of course. I overheard her the other side of the wall only last week: "You've heard from George? How is he? No, don't tell me! I have to get to Sainsbury's before it shuts. Tell me some other time. I can't stop now."

That's it, then, folks. The three great End-of-Marriage Specials on display. There's Anguish, Hate, or there's Indifference. Which one would Madam like? That's all there is.

Give Oliver his due, he did look up the minute my tears began splattering on his wrapping.

"Why are you crying, Constance? What on earth's the matter now?"

CHAPTER
EIGHT

"Why are you crying, Constance? What on earth's the matter now?"

For heaven's sake. You can't step out of one room into another in this house without finding that you have become a walk-on part in some ghastly melodrama.

"I'm not crying, Olly. These aren't tears. They're drips."

Thank God for that. I don't think I could have stood real tears this morning. Today I woke up in such a mood, such a fine mood. The early morning sun streamed through the window and hit the wall, and bounced on my face until I could actually feel my spirits rising. I got straight out of bed (that's not like me) and dressed and shaved and came downstairs while everyone else in the house was still fast asleep. I let the cat out and made a pot of tea. I even stood on the doorstep while I drank the first cup, and had a look about. The garden's very nice now. Ally has somehow managed to sort out that nasty dirt track across the grass to where the children climb over the wall into Stringbean's. The bit of fence the other side that I once set on fire by mistake has a creeper trailing over it now, hiding the scorchmarks, as well as a bush with blackcurrants or something thrusting through

178

the holes that were burned in the slats. And there are flowers in the flower beds. There never were before. Only too often when Constance was pre-menstrual she'd rip the last lot out, claiming the very sight of them made her feel sick. Then she'd buy others that would generally turn out to be the sort of plants that need more sun, or less sun, or are so downright precious they never take in the first place, never mind sun. It was a series of bare patches before good old Ally took over. He's a born gardener — keeps his eye on the seasons. Whenever he sees that time of the month hoving in view again upon the calendar, he keeps a very close watch on old Constance. And it certainly seems to have paid off. The flower beds are lovely.

After the tea, I went upstairs to work. That went well, too. With only a couple of weeks more before I leave, it was a great relief as well as a pleasure to find, today, that I was in just the right state of mind to tackle the next period in my thinking. I'd got as far as my first year back in the States after the horrors of the separation, when I finally felt the urge to take on the task of working out my own views on polyadic operations. I'd realized for some time that they were fundamentally at odds with current opinion. The issue became critical one day when I was in the classroom. I'd reached a point at which I required the notion of an arbitrary conjunction. I had wanted to explain that notion as a polyadic operation. But my sense of rigour got in the way, and I explained the notion instead in terms of its reduction to a dyadic operation.

When I left the classroom, I gave the matter some more thought. I hold it as a general methodological principle that when there is a clash between intuition and rigour — when one's sense of rigour prevents one from saying what, from an intuitive point of view, it seems that one can say — then it is rigour and not intuition that should give way. Applying this principle to the case in hand, it seemed that there should be a theory of polyadic operations upon the basis of which a satisfactory account of arbitrary conjunction and other such notions could be given. It was the attempt to develop such a theory that I'd been describing all morning, and it had come so easily you would have thought that there was someone else inside me for once, propelling it forward. None of my usual agonies about each tiny phrase: Is this clear? Is this the best word to use here? Is there no better? Could there be misunderstanding? Am I *right*?

So I had earned my coffee. But in this house, of course, there's no such thing as a free ginger nut, let alone a free lunch.

"Olly, could you just pass me another wet cloth?"

Strange thing to want. And why is Constance hunched over the table top anyway, pressing damp dishrags to her eyes? Has Ally bashed her? No, no. Impossible. If Alasdair Huggett had so much as nudged her with intent, she'd not be sitting in the kitchen wiping her eyes. She'd be upstairs, packing his bags or hers. Constance doesn't go in for the rough trade. I've biffed her once or twice, but only after she hit me first and really hurt me. She once smashed me over the head so hard with a wooden chopping board I needed fifteen stitches. The worst I've ever done, apart from simple self-defence, is pour a jug of water over her when she'd hurled herself into bed once during some row and pulled the covers up over her head to block out me (and my *very* reasonable point). She'd made such a show of being utterly distraught, it never occurred to me for a moment she'd thought to reach down surreptitiously and switch on her side of the dual electric blanket. As it turned out, the bedspread had sufficiently close weave to keep the water from seeping through, and frying her, or whatever. But you'd have thought, from the way she went on and on at me afterwards, that I was quite deliberately out to murder her. Now, if you didn't know it was impossible, you'd think that Alasdair had had a go.

Not that the fellow hasn't got his dark side. Indeed, I suspected he was in a rather ugly mood only last night, when we bumped into one another on the stairs. He gave up stepping back to let me pass a good long while ago, back in July. But I was, frankly, more than a little taken aback by his strange attitude this time. He actually seemed to get impatient at the mere sight of me rounding the corner of the landing as I headed for the stairs, holding my teacup. Usually, when we pass one another by, he opens up with something friendly and conversational: "Everything going on all right up there?" or, "The Great Autobiography coming along well?" This time, he didn't speak. I'm not a man to force someone else to make all the running. I know when it's my turn. And so I said to him as I went past: "You'll be delighted to hear things are ticking over nicely. In fact, I'm almost finished."

"Good."

He didn't sound too pleased. In fact he sounded down-right grumpy. And then he added in what I could only take to be a most accusatory tone of voice: "It's certainly taken long enough. You've been up in that attic nearly twelve weeks. You must have much more of a past than I do."

"And much more of a future."

I said it lightly enough, as I went by. But when Constance suddenly peeled off her wet cloth and I saw her horribly swollen and blackened eye, I had serious doubts about whether I shouldn't have resisted the temptation.

"Christ! That is awful, Constance. You look an absolute fright. What on earth happened?"

"Poor Ally sloshed me."

Mystery! If I had done that, she'd be out the house and down the Women's Refuge by now, dialling the cops, and hectoring them mightily on her civil rights if they didn't immediately offer to rustle up a posse of armed men to come and flush me out of house and home. Alasdair Huggett gets to slosh her round the chops, and he remains the object of her tender sympathy. You have to hand it to the fellow. Ratbag aside, he certainly has a way with women.

"But that's terrible, Constance. Whatever did you say to provoke him?"

She glared — a rather drippy and inadequate one-eyed glare. But still a glare.

"I didn't say anything, Oliver. Or do anything. I simply slept peacefully on my pillow while Ally rolled over in bed yelling "Damn you, Stella!" and landed his fist in my eye. Then I woke up."

"Alasdair must have felt dreadful."

Scowling, Constance returned her attention to her sophisticated dishcloth after-care. Realizing I'd put a foot wrong, I tried again.

"Mind you, I didn't think that he was in the best of moods. He was quite short with me yesterday on the landing, I thought."

"He's not been sleeping well."

Too right he hasn't, flailing his great fists about like some gigantic rotary whisk, punching his beloved's lights out. The trouble with Ally, of course, is that he takes things far too much to heart. He's one of those soft souls who go round believing, right down deep inside, that everything ought to work out fine and dandy. People like him are self-primed for disappointment. Those who take my more robust view of the world and all its evil works are in a better position in the end. We may not spend our days whistling quite so chirpily as Alasdair Huggett. But on the day the bombs drop, the pogroms start, the last forests vanish, at least we won't be leaning on our spades, grappling with astonishment and disillusion. We'll be the ones already under the table, discussing which of us saw it coming first.

Still, everyone to his own way of getting through the years. Perhaps Ally had drifted off down the bottom of the garden to plant hemlock.

"Where is the Midnight Mauler, anyway? Why isn't he here on his knees, begging your pardon and bathing your raw wounds?"

Constance narrowed her eyes. Then, wincing with pain, stopped bothering, and answered amiably enough:

"He's just slipped off to see Ned."

"Really? Judging by the damage the man's done to your face practising, Stella had better watch out."

"He won't be seeing her. Ned's not at home. Ratbag's gone back to work today, so Ned's been sentenced to a week at Gosworthy Road Primary School Holiday Project."

"Is Ally springing him?"

"It's not a prison, Oliver. It's an urban day-care facility. Ally couldn't get him out of there in a million years."

"So what's he doing? Poking buns through the bars?"

"Something like that. He sits one side of the railings and Ned sits the other. Then they hold hands and chat."

"Really?"

"Yes. Really."

Silence. And then I gave my Constance a very good, hard, long look. She can't fool me.

"Those aren't drips, Constance. Those are proper tears."

Oh, no. She can't fool me.

I was still thinking about it as I went back up the stairs. It all seemed such a waste. Here we have sun and fresh air, juicy green grass (now Ally's coped with it), and large tracts of the house knee-deep in toys. I've been to Gosworthy Road. Bonnie went to that school for two whole terms the year Constance went too far too fast in her crusade against sexism in Wallisdean Primary. It is an urban slum. There is one big tree in the middle of the yard, but none of the children are permitted to touch it. It has spiked railings around it to keep them off.

184

Not the place to spend the last week of your summer. Not if you have a choice. And Ned should have the option. Apart from worshipping his father like a god (sees him as rarely as the average Briton goes to church, of course), he gets on well enough with everyone in this house. I know there was a time I used to get a bit testy, when sometimes it seemed I could scarcely round a corner in my own home without catching my foot in his trailing wet nappies. But once he was up on his pins I didn't mind him at all. Not that I've seen that much of him the last few years, since his father's Great Marital Defection. But on the few occasions he has been allowed round here, he's always seemed to fit in. Charges around the place squealing merrily enough, with Nancy at his heels. Turns down the sound on the telly if you thump on the floor. Doesn't mess with my papers. A lot less trouble than the other two, in fact. And it's a crying shame that he can't spend more time with them. Nancy adores him (Stringbean goes quite green) and Bonnie's good to him. I can remember one particular afternoon when he was in distress about his sums. For some reason he couldn't fathom subtraction, and was upset because he'd fallen so far behind in his workbook that some of the little monsters in his class had taken to jeering at him in the playground. "Remeejals! Remeejals! Ned's going to have to go to Remeejals!"

My playground miseries are not so misted up by time I have forgotten them entirely. "Listen," I told him. "The whole thing is perfectly simple. Let me explain."

I was right in the middle of a perfectly adequate explanation of what subtraction is, and how it operates, when Bonnie forcibly interposed herself between me and Ned.

"Don't listen to *him*," she said scornfully. "*He* doesn't know. I'll tell you how to do it."

Don't listen to *him* — he doesn't know. Oh, you can hear her mother in that, can't you, clear as a temple bell. My peers repeatedly refer to me as one of the finest mathematical logicians alive. They take me for a dumbo. It drives me wild!

And I was doubly appalled by what I heard. It was unspeakable. Sheer mathematical carnage. A midden of conceptual error and sentimental whimsy. "Now you haven't got enough, have you? So you're going to have to trot straight round next door, and borrow from nice Mrs Hundreds." "Don't forget to pay back kind Mr Tens, after he was so good to you and lent you some." "There aren't enough of the baby ones, are there? No. So what are they going to have to do? That's right! Borrow!"

It made me ill to listen. I was outraged.

"It's no use him just *doing* it," I argued with Bonnie. "He shouldn't just be learning some mindless technique, parrot-fashion. He has to grasp the concept of place-value first. He has to *understand*."

"No, he doesn't," said Bonnie. "He just has to *do* it."

Ned clearly took her part. And so did Alasdair. Constance, of course, has never held with sums. I was shooed off, unspeakably dispirited about the state of mathematics teaching in British primary schools. The single bright spot, looking back on things, is that Ned somehow caught on in a flash, and stayed well clear of "Remeejals'.

Proving my family does have something to offer. There's no need for this peevishness on Ratbag's part. She only does it to spite Ally. I would advise him to go back to court, but I've heard quite enough of the results of that filtering up the pipes over the years. As far as I can make out, courts are as useless at assuring the rights of fathers as they are at winkling maintenance out of most of them. It's only when the summonses are heaped knee-deep on her doormat that Ratbag even bothers to hand in one or another of the sick notes and excuses she forged in bulk that time she was ordered into Conciliation (Stella's conception of what it is to be conciliatory turning out to equal in sheer distortion Constance's notion of marriage guidance, which was to turn up once a week to loll about in a comfortable chair, urging some counsellor to browbeat me).

You have to hand it to Ally's lawyer, though. He's fully Stella's match in dilatoriness, if not in actual wits. Between the causes for further delay furnished first by the one, then by the other, week after week crawls by. Ally gets wild-eyed, waiting. Ned sniffs the wind, and gnaws his fingernails so hard blood seeps round the edges if he so much as presses his knife into a slice of spam. And each time the issue of Huggett vs Huggett struggles out into daylight for an hour or so, the only professionals at hand seem to be brain-soft social workers determined to give poor Mrs Ratbag one last chance, and grim busy men of law who practically wonder aloud in court what sort of pervert this Mr Huggett must be to want to see more of his own child than they see of theirs. Stella looks anxious and cooperative — and rather fetching in her nice blue outfit. At the first sight of her, Ally promptly forgets all Constance's detailed stage directions and starts to glower in a fashion so menacing it fails to further his already dubious suit. And Little Ned, if called on to air his wishes confidentially behind closed doors, takes care to stare neutrally at his freshly polished shoe-caps and answer every question with the one thing he knows won't bring the sky down on his head. And that, of course, is "Don't know."

I'd have a wife's ears off if she tried those games on me. I'd starve her out. Ally behaves like an ex-marital wimp, posting his monthly cheques as regular as clockwork, and trying to justify his spineless submission to injustice with talk of "not sinking to Stella's level" and "putting Ned's feelings first". I don't know how the man can do it. I'd rather slit my throat. Constance can point out (as she so tartly did last night when Ned had, yet again, failed to show up) that, as with the story of King Solomon and the rival mothers, it is the baby in the bacon slicer, not the two litigants. It would be Ned's blood on the floor, not mine. But I wouldn't let that put me off for an instant. After all, right is right. I'd never let myself end up like Alasdair, watching clocks, staring bitterly at calendars, starting up hopefully at telephones and doorbells. And thumping people feverishly in my sleep.

At least he sleeps now. That's a bit of an advance. I can remember one particular Christmas Eve when I was kept awake all bloody night by the sound of him snivelling in the next bedroom. I would have ousted

Bonnie, if I'd thought. Her bedroom's miles away, across the stairs. But I'd not banked on sleeping in the house at all. There was no bed made up. So when Constance unaccountably rushed from the sitting room in floods of tears, leaving me marooned in a sea of unwrapped presents, I had to sort things out as best I could. First I finished the job in hand. The Christmas Bunnies looked a little odd, what with clotted bits of sticky tape all over their wheelbarrows and tear-stains running down their tartan trews. And I confess that, after a while, I did lose track a bit of what was what. One present looks very much like another once you've wrapped two or three layers around it to try and hide the rips in the paper. I wasn't at all sure about the one lying behind me on the floor, for example. Was it Bonnie's? Or Nancy's? But since, in any case, I heard it crunch a bit beneath my foot as I stood up, it probably wasn't going to matter anyway. So I simply stuffed it, along with everything else, down one or another of the enormous red velvet feet-shaped things you might think Constance deliberately ran up on her sewing machine to foster our pampered children's seasonal spasms of greed, and, finished at last, I shoved the bloody things away under a chair, out of the way of the marauding cat. Free to go off to bed! Nancy's the lightest, so it was her I scooped up and carried across the landing to her sister's room, and tipped into the bed.

Bonnie, of course, has inherited her mother's gift for sitting up and grumbling in her sleep.

"You can't put Nancy in with me! The stockings will get all mixed up!"

"Don't be so silly," I said, tucking Nancy in firmly beside her. "Go back to sleep. You can worry about sorting out your clothes in the morning."

It's no mean feat, sleeping in Nancy's bed. So far as I can make out, the only reason for not flinging it on a corporation tip at once is that it serves some custodial purpose. Once in, you can't get out. It's like a ditch. I lay clamped firmly down each side, scarcely able to stir, and listened willy-nilly as, through the wall, came sounds of Ally sobbing. It was horrible. And, as that mercifully wore away, snatches of everything that followed: the quite outrageous row he picked with Constance for neglecting him all Christmas Eve in favour of myself; her spirited defence; their furtive bonk; and then, when Constance finally climbed back into bed after, as she so offensively put it, "scouring the entire house for the stockings that mad mongo hid under some chair", their long, long conversation about Ned.

"She could have let him *phone*."

"Mean troll! Your turn for the fourth Christmas in a row, and she just does it *again*."

"I honestly didn't believe she'd have the nerve. Not after what happened last year."

"I hope Ned doesn't try those sort of hunger-strike tactics again."

"If he does, that will be the third year in a row he's missed his Christmas dinner."

"And half his presents."

"Presents! Oh, Christ! I knew I should have played safe and given them to him last time he came."

"He didn't come last time. If he had, we might have managed to work out what she had up her sleeve."

190

"She can't have slunk off to Wales. She and her mother still aren't speaking after last year. So where the hell has the miserable bat gone? I rang all day, you know. Seven this morning until ten tonight. And I went round there twice. Either she's spirited the poor little bugger away, or she's unplugged her telephone and they're sitting in the pitch dark!"

"And no note for the milkman?"

"Ned says she's rumbled that one."

"Pity. Reading those notes has saved an awful lot of time . . ."

"And worry . . ."

"Yes . . .

It went on — and on and on and on. I couldn't sleep. I think that Nancy's eiderdown must be some sort of toy one. It's very short. It barely covered my feet. What I couldn't work out is how the two of them could lie there hour after hour, churning out factory fresh outrage. They must have known that, on past form alone, Ned's festive abduction was to be expected. People don't change. I tried to say as much to Constance once, during some marital wrangle. In fact, I only got as far as "You'll never change", and she went wholly berserk. It was extraordinary. I've never seen her so angry in my life. She turned into a Fury on the spot. "Bastard! You shitty creep! I've twisted myself completely out of shape over the last ten years, trying to satisfy you! How *dare* you? Pig! Bastard! Blind, ungrateful turd!"

Her eyes were burning and her face was white. But she was wrong, wrong, wrong. She hadn't changed a bit over the years. Sensing right from the start that one side of me strongly disliked one side of her, she'd tried. But she had failed. And that was that. And nothing since has ever led me to believe she's capable of change in any way. Year after year she treats me exactly the same. "Oliver, are you getting up in time for lunch, or aren't you?" "Don't leave your stuff there, please. Clear it away." "Shouldn't you go off to bed now? Even if you can't sleep?" (Truly, this jet-lag business is a perfect curse.) Still shows me no consideration at all. Still makes no allowance whatever for the fact that, very probably, in order to get on the plane at all, I have been busy night and day, marking my students' papers, checking proofs, and meeting all New Year deadlines in advance. Naturally when I arrive in Britain I am exhausted. Is it so bad of me to need more than one call when, after keeping me awake all night with noisy sobbing through the wall, she and Ally want to drag me out of bed in the morning?

"Olly! It's after twelve! If you don't get up soon, there won't be time to open any presents before lunch."

"Olly! It's half-past twelve!"

"Olly! It's one!"

Finally, she lets the dogs loose. Bonnie comes first. "It's terribly selfish of you, lounging around in bed like this. We're all bored stiff, waiting to open our stuff. And Ally's worried that his turkey's shrivelling."

". . . go ahead . . . not wait for me . . . don't mind . . ."

"Nancy won't. Not without you. Why can't you just get up? It's two o'clock."

". . . not to me, it isn't . . . six in the morning . . ."

"Well, that's your problem."

192

(It was Constance who taught them both that one. Apart from almost the entire contents of this laundry cupboard and three Shaker chairs, it was the only thing about America that delighted her so much she went to the trouble of bringing it back with her.)

Nancy was next. She burst in: "Don't shave! Dad-*dee*! Don't start to shave!" and burst out: "Mum! Now he's shaving! Stop him shaving, *please*!"

Constance just pops her head around the door long enough to say, "Olly, it's quarter past two! Ally can only hold the turkey off for so long. Are you nearly ready?"

Ally contents himself with opening doors and wafting lunch smells at me.

"A Merry Christmas, Oliver! Large gin and tonic?"

"God, no. I'll stick with tea while I'm eating my toast, thanks."

"Toast?" Nancy goes careering through the downstairs rooms in search of Constance. "Mum! Mum! Now he says he's having *breakfast*! You've got to stop him! Please! We'll *never* get our presents!"

I'm not at my best in the mornings, Constance knows that. If she sails in here and tries her Nanny act on me, she'll find I'll just chew slower.

In she comes.

"Oliver, I do think if only for the children's sake you should try and make more of an effort to get back on the right time."

"Right time." Get that? Britannia Rules the Waves.

"For Christ's sake, Constance. It's only *dawn* for me. I need the bloody tea to wake me up."

"Well, get on and bloody make it!"

"Don't rush me. Don't *rush* me."

Snarl, snarl. We might as well still be married. She'll never change. Few things in families do. The Christmas rituals are just the same. I get my annual brace of shirts from her. She gets expensive perfume (duty-free) and chocolates from me. He gives her chocolates too (which makes me think that, behind doors, he gave her something silkier and much more private). The children give me socks, him bulbs and seeds. He gives me a toilet bag (a little hint that he'd like back the one I borrowed last year). I give him aftershave (yes, duty-free). She gives him a nice woolly. The children do so well a vague unease about the whole affair spreads round the three of us as their loot piles grow higher and higher. The room fills up with crumpled glittery paper. The cat goes mad. And Ally will keep going on about his bloody turkey. I never see the problem, personally. It always works out fine. The turkey turns up on the table cooked. So do the roast potatoes and the sprouts. The sausages are done. The gravy's hot. Where is the need for fretting? Ally can count. He's not innumerate, like Constance. I can see why she can't do Christmas dinner — never could. She is incapable of the simple feat of working out how long each item takes to cook and starting it off at the right time. That's why I always did the Sunday lunch (and, I've no doubt, why Ally does it now). Left to the mercy of her own primitive methods of calculation (fingers and worried staring at the clock) Constance's roasts used to stretch through entire afternoons, as first the meat was done, and then the pudding ready, and, later, the spuds began to soften up a bit just at the moment when the

194

sprouts turned out perfect. "Listen," I said to her one day when she was standing frowning at Nancy's digital watch and toiling with the (you would think) not overly taxing concept of twenty-seven minutes to the pound plus twenty-seven minutes if it's on the bone, thirty-five otherwise. "It's perfectly simple —"

She threw the sprouts at me. I changed my tack.

"I know," I said. "You wash and peel and stuff the things, and I'll tell you when to start cooking them. How about that?"

"Oh, Olly!" She flung her arms around me. She was radiant. "Angel! You are so sweet!" You'd think it was the Relief of Mafeking. There was real adoration in her eyes. Pure gratitude. Love.

She doesn't need me now. Ally can run the show perfectly well. The turkey is delicious. I have thirds. And, after, I listen to him cope with the organization of the clearing-up with none of those rumblings of resentment and recrimination about whose turn it really is to load the dishwasher or scour the pans echoing up the pipes to mar the afternoon peace. The man works miracles — is, in himself, the perfect Christmas gift. I've learned to leave the whole lot up to him. They're better off without me. He knows best. I think that Ally was, at first, in his artless and rather inarticulate homespun way, a little chary about wellying straight in at times of domestic disaster to cope with my wife and daughters in front of me. But I don't mind at all. My self-esteem has never been invested in my skills as a husband or parent. If he can handle things better than me, good luck to the man. I'm on his side. Frankly, I'd just as soon sit up here in the laundry room, in peace, having a quiet little think, as spend the whole of Christmas afternoon trying to mollify an exhausted and disgruntled child about the disappointments of the day.

"It doesn't fit. It hurts — here — and it's *scratchy*. It makes me itch. I *hate* it. I'm going to take it off and never wear it!"

"Fold it up neatly, Nancy, and we'll take it back to the shop."

"Can you take the felt pens back, too? They're the wrong sort. I wanted pointy ones, and these are *thick*."

I'd snap at that point. Tell the ungrateful little baggage to stop her whining at once. But Ally has the patience of a saint.

"I'll chum you upstairs, shall I? Then you can tell me everything that's wrong with all your presents while I slip you into your nightie for a little nap, so you can stay up really late tonight, watching telly."

I reckon the fellow might even have succeeded, too, if Bonnie hadn't been round the room once too often, sipping from everyone's glass.

"Her felt pens aren't the only things round here that are thick."

Nancy burst into tears. After a second or two, the sound of her sobbing was partially muffled. Ally must have picked her up in his arms, to carry her upstairs. There was the most tremendous bang as Nancy somehow managed to kick the door, presumably in Bonnie's face, as Ally swept her out. There was a short hiatus as I heard nothing further up the pipes, and then the sound of their voices floated round the corner of the landing.

196

"I want Victoria Plum. I haven't seen Victoria Plum for ages. I want Victoria Plum now."

"Promise me you'll sleep?"

The laundry-room door opened. Ally stood on the threshold like some gigantic vision of St Christopher, Nancy still in his arms.

"I'm sorry, Oliver. Nancy needs Victoria Plum."

I am mystified.

"There's no-one else in here."

Ally explained.

"It's a pillowcase, Oliver. It must be in the cupboard behind you."

"Oh. Right."

"Pink," Nancy said sourly, lifting her head from Ally's chest just long enough to reveal an unappealing slug trail from her nose running up Ally's sleeve. "With pretty hearts and flowers."

I rooted cooperatively about inside the laundry cupboard for a bit. The only pink hearts and flowers I could see were on one of the things I was keeping a few sheets of paper in for safety. She'd better not have that.

"Sorry. Can't find it."

"You've got to! You've got to! Find it, Daddy! Now!"

Not having that. Oh, no. Alasdair may have more sensitivity and show more tact, but my view is that children ought to hear the truth about themselves when their behaviour is appalling.

"Now just you listen to me, Nance —"

But she was snivelling again, moaning and weeping, and wiping her nose down Ally's sleeve.

"Nancy! Nance! Stop it! Stop making that unholy row. Stop acting like a brat!"

"Easy," warned Alasdair. "She's had a difficult day."

"Difficult day?" I couldn't believe my ears. "Difficult *day*? What's difficult about stuffing your face with food and squatting on heaps of expensive presents?"

Nance gave me a simply poisonous look.

"The dress was *scratchy*. And the felt pens were *thick*."

I lost my patience, I'm afraid, at that point.

"What about your bloody Christmas stocking? That giant loot bag was stuffed to the gills with goodies. I bet they weren't all too scratchy or too thick! What about them?"

Her eyes flash, and she's pointing at me now. Still in her primary school, and looks just like her mother. "I hope you know my stocking wasn't any good! I hope you know it didn't have hardly anything in it that I like. I hope you know that what I like in my stocking is Magic Bubbles and chocolate coins, and what I like to do is sit up in my bed and eat my chocolate coins and blow my Magic Bubbles and wait for Stringbean to phone and tell me what she got. And *someone* went and put me in the wrong bed so the stockings got all mixed up and Bonnie snatched all the good things. And *someone* had trodden on the Magic Bubbles pot so it had leaked on everything and the chocolate coins tasted all slimy and horrible like washing-up stuff, and Mum had to take them off me in case I was sick. And all I got in my stocking that wasn't ruined was this stupid thing!"

And she held out the gift I had gone to the trouble of unpacking the entire contents of two whole suitcases to find and wrap at one in the morning.

198

"It still works, doesn't it? I certainly hope it does. It cost enough."

"I don't know if it works, do I? I don't even know what it does. The stupid thing hasn't even got any batteries!"

No batteries. Felled at a stroke. The classic Christmas blunder — no batteries. I am not cut out for this family lark at all. Giving me a look (God knows what sort of look — it was a look so deeply impenetrable I didn't even know if it was to do with me or with Nancy), Alasdair heaved the thrashing bulk of my furious daughter further up over his shoulder, and carried her off out of sight. A merciful release. This Christmas business is a perfect nightmare. It chews up everything. It wears me down. I am no good at buying toys and little things for girls. I stood for hours at that bloody counter in Placid City, trying to choose between the blue one with the jumping dogs and the red one with piglets. When the saleswoman offered me batteries I said no because I knew hers were a perfect fiddle at twice the price of a supermarket pack. Then I forgot. Yes, I forgot. Hang me! I'm guilty. I forgot the batteries! But it was not my fault. I warned Constance all those bloody years ago that I was not the right man for the job. She took her chances having both the kids. It should be she who ends up paying the price, not me. But I end up the victim. Look what has happened to me, for heaven's sake. I am sucked into something I never wanted in the first place. Dependencies I never asked for grow on me until I actually *like* having a house, a home, two kids, a body in the bed, someone who's always there. And then what?

She throws me out! It takes her several horrible, miserable, guilt-ridden years, but she still does it. And they were horrible, miserable, guilt-ridden years for me, too, don't forget. Years of feeling on the edge of things. Years of being slowly, steadily pushed out. I'm made dispensable and made to feel that it is all my fault. But it's not fair. If I'm not what she wanted, then she should never have married me in the first place. And, since she did, she should know what it cost. It cost a *lot*. I never thought I'd live with anyone. I vowed I wouldn't. Hadn't I seen enough, as I grew up, to know it interferes the whole bloody time? Ask around. Ask anyone with brains and ambition. Old Dante knew: "He who knows most, grieves most for wasted time." He knew. He knew how, once people like Constance move in, people like me with dreams and aspirations don't find the time to work on them very much longer. First it's one thing, then another. Eating together, outings, noisy Hoovers round your feet, people to dinner (as if you didn't see enough of bloody people), talking about them afterwards (as if the evening hadn't lasted long enough). "What did you think of her, then?" "What about him?" "Did you think that the fish was cooked right?" "I really liked her jacket." Then children! Years of nerve-racking, intellect-draining children. You come to care for them. They care for you. It gets to matter to you, even, when they burst into tears about some stupid, childish disappointment like Magic Bubbles on their chocolate coins. What a pity your wife so recently, out of the blue, found someone much more suitable for the job, and suddenly deciding that merely grousing about your great personal inadequacies wasn't

200

good enough, heaved you out like some old unwanted mattress, to go for something better, more her style. At least you're free, perhaps? Free to revert to that pure, simple, previously imagined life. No. Sorry. That option's off now, I'm afraid. You see there is a small child over there — a small child pointing at you accusingly with tears of rage and disappointment in her eyes. You are not free at all. You never will be. You have to think about the fucking batteries.

I can't contend with this lot. I want out. Left to myself, I have the strength and power of twenty men. Put me in this house and I become as helpless and enfeebled as that French poet's poor bloody albatross, staggering about the ship's deck: "How can he walk, for he has giant's wings?" How can I get up when they do, go tidily off to bed when it suits them? I cannot work that way. You can't keep tight rein on a working mind. At night it slips out of gear. I find myself awake in the early hours. My thoughts spin round. Splinters of yesterday's thinking race about uncontrollably, careering into bits of what I want to think about tomorrow. I try to slow things down, but it's impossible. Nothing will still my brain, and I try everything. (You'd think the mere thought of Debbie taking off her clothes would bring an entire railway network, not just my few haphazard trains of thought, successfully screeching to a halt. But, on these nights, before the little lovely's even down to her slip, my mind's off and away, back on whatever it is I'm trying to iron out, get to the bottom of, *get straight*.) Maybe around five in the morning I might get off to sleep at last.

So I rise late. So I rise late! So what? So bloody what? They get along well enough without me most of the year, they make that perfectly clear. So why should it suddenly be such a big issue that I want to lie in? Why am I supposed to feel guilty? I tell you, it is a Nietzschean Act of Will not to be sucked down by guilt when you live on the same planet as Constance, let alone in the same house. This woman is walking quicksand, an emotional swamp. You have to hold firm, or you'll go straight under. You take last Christmas. When I left this house, I felt pretty good. All the way to the airport I felt better and better. Partly because I was getting away again, of course. But partly the cheerfulness and self-esteem that comes from a job well done, a task achieved. Enjoyed the children. Got on well enough with Ally. Not fought too much with her. When Constance pulled up the car outside Departures, I leaped out and swung my suitcases out of the back, then turned to give her a friendly farewell kiss.

"Well," I said. "That's it, then." I waved a hand to indicate the recent past. "I think it was worth it for the children. Pity they didn't manage to wake up in time to see me off. I thought Nancy loved airports. But never mind."

Constance glanced up at the clock-face on the airport tower.

"I just hope I can get them back on British time before term starts . . ."

See? Her little poisoned farewell gift. I bring her duty-free. She gives me guilt. Well, bugger her. Damned if I'll crawl around apologizing for things like forgetting

202

batteries and sleeping in. Really the woman is impossible. Guilt is for married men. She threw me out.

And I am leaving. I have had enough. In fact, I'm going to shove this back in the airing cupboard right now, and go up and finish that bloody thing for Fairbairn. Then I am getting out. I shall be glad to get away from them, their endless tears and drips and blackened eyes, their worries about children, their constant bloody meals. I'm sick of family life. The only value in it was its permanence, and they took that away.

They don't need me at all. I'm getting out.

CHAPTER
NINE

"Olly! Can you come down, please? We need you."

Cheek!

I push the attic door open just enough to bellow down the stairs. "I'm busy, Constance. I'm busy finishing this thing you all so much want me to finish, So, whatever it is, get your Alasdair to do it."

Great ringing guffaws from the kitchen.

"No. Ally won't do. We need you, Oliver."

So much for not being needed. Sighing, I push aside the great stack of pages written for Fairbairn, the Great Piano Usurer, and, stacking up the coffee mugs and teacups that wouldn't fit on Nancy's tray when Constance sent her up on the last trawl, I come downstairs to see just what it is that Oliver Rosen, and only Oliver Rosen, can do for them today.

"Well?"

"Oh, Olly. Don't be so grumpy. It won't take a minute. And, anyway, you get a treat from it."

"What sort of treat?"

"A slice of blackcurrant tart."

Nancy's great passion. I turn and wink at her. But she is sitting in a small black cloud. So I turn back to Constance.

"And what must I do to earn my slice of tart?"

Constance grins.

"Share it out fairly."

My eyes go round the table. Aren't there enough of them to share out their own bloody treats and send me some up quietly on a tray, with one more cup of tea? There's Ally, Constance, Bonnie, Nancy and even Stringbean around the table on which are sitting two enormous glistening black tarts, one either side of that daft cow jug Constance bought in Leek and — rarity of rarities these days — the great big sugar bowl.

Teatime indeed!

"Pass the knife, then."

Solemnly Alasdair hands across the long sharp knife, and that peculiar silver-plated trowel my former mother-in-law once put me out by giving me for Christmas.

"Right, then. Into six?"

Ally spoke up.

"You don't mind making it seven, do you, Oliver? Just in case Ned turns up later." He glanced round helplessly. "You never know . . ."

I know. And Constance knows. And everyone else around this table, even Stringbean, knows. But if he wants to cling to his pathetic little fantasies, that is his problem.

"Seven. Right."

I lift the knife. This time it's Bonnie's voice ringing out that stops me.

"Not just *plain* sevens."

"Sevenths," I corrected her. "We're dealing here in fractions."

"We knew you were our man!" Constance crowed. "Fractions! That is exactly what we want. But not just plain old sevens —"

"Sevenths."

"Sevenths." (She's such a numerical non-starter, she barely manages to get her tongue around the word.) "We don't want plain old sevenths." She glanced across the table at Nancy, who was still deeply sunk in the dark mulligrubs. "Nancy wants something fairer."

I raised an eyebrow at Nance.

"You realize that sevenths are equal?" I tentatively asked her.

"She wants something fairer than equal!" hooted Bonnie.

I was still watching Nance.

"Fairer than equal? That is what you want?"

Ignoring the grinning around her, she nodded sullen assent.

"Yes. I want fairer than equal."

Fairer than equal, says the philosopher's daughter. I felt a sudden rush of satisfaction. A glorious shaft of love. My blood and bone! The only person in this house who truly needs me, soon might understand, and has to know that there are others out there in the world who think as she does, and have come to see the limitations of sloppy and complacent everyday thinking. People who want to dig deeper, find the truth. Oh, no. The apple does not fall far from the tree. We let the food go cold upon the table back there at 73 Nitshill Road, fighting about fair shares. Finn and Sol (just representatives of "his" and "hers') would fish the rusty serving implements out of the kitchen drawer, and, as whoever won the toss sank the point of the compass into the top of the pie, the rest of us would argue frantically about whether the protractor had swivelled surreptitiously a little to the left, or, more fundamentally, about what compensation should be paid for gobbets of pastry still congealed, or parts of pie cooked far beyond recognition. The host of special effects created by an oven salvaged off the local tip fuelled all our calculating skills, and raised the larger questions. Did burn count? For Gerry, perhaps. He was content to eat clinker. But Joe and Finn picked off the blackened bits before they started. Should they be given more to make things "fair"?

And now my younger child had realized the serious, the crippling limitations of "equal". She hadn't simply taken against it in the deeply irritating knee-jerk way her mother did over the years of our marriage — sometimes it seemed to me the very word had come to symbolize for Constance all that she hated most about my work. It had become a red rag to a bull. She loathed it. It provoked her beyond measure. "What's your view on all this, Olly?" she'd ask mildly enough, sitting up in bed eating cheese crackers and lime pickle, and watching some mealy-mouthed governmental crawler on the television spew out the party line on some issue of the moment. "Well," I'd say guardedly. "All things being equal —" She'd never hear the rest. She'd have gone mad. "All things *aren't* equal!" she would yell at me. "Never are! Never were! Never bloody will be! I'm not

207

asking if, all things being equal, you agree with the brown-nosed little creep! I'm asking if you *do*!"

But I can't help it. I am not like her. Spouting is not my style. I need "all things being equal". Philosophers do. *Ceteris paribus*. It is bedrock for thought, the base camp from which all philosophical excursions must start. Work out how things aren't equal, and light pours in. And now my Nance had suddenly seen equality does not necessarily bring justice in its train. By her own lights, she had begun the long, determined search for truth.

"Nancy," I said. "Have you a special sort of 'fair' in mind?"

She couldn't have looked blanker. I explained.

"You see, there are several ways that we could go about this. We could, after some discussion, try to prorate the portions of this tart in accordance with all the effort put into gathering together the ingredients and making it; or we could let the division depend upon the hunger levels of the recipients, though that would be a lot more difficult to assess. Easier, perhaps, to allot shares by virtue of the various relevant body weights."

She was still looking blank. I soldiered on.

"Or we could do it, perhaps, on simple utilitarian grounds: work out who gets most pleasure out of eating tart —"

Her eyes lit up. The others shouted "No!"

"Or," I said, tacking out of choppy water, "we could do the whole thing in a far more basic fashion. For example, we could calculate it proportionately, by age —"

208

"Dad!" Bonnie bellowed. "It is getting cold!" She turned to snarl at her sister. "You're the one who wants it cutting differently. So hurry up and decide!"

(There it is, should you ever want it: the hallmark of the slovenly thinker — haste.)

Nancy, meantime, was looking quite nonplussed, like someone who has lifted up a stone and found a thriving colony underneath of something she never knew existed, and isn't sure she likes. But, in the face of Bonnie's irritation, she hastily picked up the last of my suggestions.

"Do it by age."

"Proportionately, by age? Are you quite sure?"

"Nancy, you are not going to like this," warned Constance.

Nancy's sheer stubborness propelled her. "I'm older than Stringbean. And I'm older than Ned."

"On the other hand," I said, "you're —"

"Get on with it, Daddy!" roared Bonnie. "I'm fed up with waiting. We're all fed up with waiting. Cut the pie. If Nancy's mean enough to want one more blackcurrant than Stringbean, then what she gets is her silly problem!"

It was, I thought, a most uncharitable interpretation of the confusions that attend stirrings of abstract thought. But, on the other hand, knowledge gleaned through experience can bring lasting insight.

"Right, then," I said. "At Nancy's request, the cutting of this tart is going to be proportionate, by age."

I raised the knife for the third time.

"No, Olly," Constance said. "You'd better not. It's going to end in tears."

"I don't care how it turns out," Nance said defiantly.

"Get *on* with it!" begged Bonnie.

"I have to go soon," Stringbean announced. "It's nearly time for my tea."

"Oh, go on, Oliver," Constance snapped. She was quite suddenly sick of children, you could tell. "Just go ahead and cut the bloody thing!"

"First," I said, "I am going to need some additional data."

I glanced enquiringly at Alasdair.

"If you must know," he said. "I'm forty-two."

I didn't rub it in.

"Right, then," I said. "Ally is forty-two and I'm two years younger. Constance is younger than me by the same amount again. Nancy is three years younger than Bonnie, and one year older than Stringbean; but since her birthday falls so soon, I'm going to make it two. And then we have to add on Ned, of course, who, by my calculations has to be two years younger than Stringbean. So that makes exactly one hundred and fifty-nine years into three hundred and sixty, which is about as close to two point three —"

"Wait a minute," broke in Ally. "Why three hundred and sixty?"

He looked quite mystified.

"Degrees," I patiently explained.

"In a blackcurrant tart?"

I stared. But Ally, it was obvious, was just as horrified as I was. "Would you like a protractor?" he asked with leaden sarcasm. "Or a —" (The fact that he had to be openly prompted by Bonnie here robbed his taunt, I thought, of a good deal of its punch.) "Or a compass?"

"That won't be necessary," I said frostily, and I admit that I showed off outrageously in the speed of the cutting: "So, starting with the smallest, we have approximately sixteen point one degrees of tart for Ned — not really worth keeping, actually, Ally, when you come to look at it. And not very much more, only twenty point seven degrees, for Stringbean — I must say it's a very good job you're going straight home for another tea. And twenty-three degrees exactly for Nancy — I'm sorry, but you did decide to do it this way and it is fair, well, fair proportionately by age, at least."

She stared at the tiny, leaking lump on her dish, then glowered horribly at me. But I pressed bravely on.

"Twenty-nine point nine degrees for Bonnie — and perhaps if you hadn't rushed your sister so unpleasantly, she might have changed her mind about how to dish it up fairly, and you might have ended up with a whole lot more. And eighty-seven point four degrees for Constance — I can't pretend I'll be sorry if it sticks in your throat and chokes you after you've dragged me away from my work just to fetch me up in the doghouse with Nancy." The knife sheared cleanly through the remaining half of the tart. "Ninety-two degrees for me, I think — lovely, I must say it looks quite delicious. I think those blackcurrants that rolled over there are mine." And, on to the last dish: "Ninety-six point six degrees, the biggest slice of all, for Alasdair — because he's the *oldest*."

I handed it over with a flourish.

"There," I announced, looking round satisfied. "I think that's all quite fair."

Ally said bolshily: "Is that some sort of Rosen family grace? Should we be saying 'Amen'?" He looked down at his slice of tart. For all his portion was the biggest, he didn't seem too pleased. Neither did anyone else around the table. Stringbean haughtily tipped her tiny little teaspoonful into her mouth, and rose at once to leave. Bonnie turned to glower at Nancy. Nancy's eyes filled with tears. And then, of course, Ally and Constance had to busy themselves carving great hunks off their own bits and hastily passing them over to the children.

I poured cream on to mine.

"Delicious. Perfect. Very nice indeed."

I can't say they put themselves out to be chatty. The tea was over in the time it took for each of them to shovel their helping off their plates and into their mouths, and, following Stringbean's example, get up to go.

Ally was first.

"Has it stopped raining? I think I might just stroll down Gosworthy Road, and see if by any chance Ned's been let out in the compound."

Constance was on her feet at once.

"Don't bother smuggling that stupid slice in. You give him this." Snatching up the knife, she carved a huge wedge from the second tart, and slid it on to the paper plate Ally had fetched from the cupboard.

Without thinking, Nancy just burst out with it:

"That isn't *fair*!"

212

Her sister snickered. Nance turned to swipe her round the head, and missed. Then, all the frustrations of a disappointing teatime exploding, she ran, howling horribly, out of the room.

Constance trained her maternal sights on Bonnie.

"That was your fault!"

I didn't stay to hear the argument. I slipped away upstairs, back to my work. And any nastiness couldn't have lasted for long, because when I slid the upstairs toilet window open only a few minutes later, I saw the two of them together in the garden. Constance was working her way along the fence, filling one of her everlasting punnets. And Bonnie was scolding her in a return match.

"You shouldn't have to do this. It's ridiculous. Picking berries just to throw them away! You ought to tell next door to pull their stupid bush back on their own side."

"I couldn't. Since your father burned all those giant holes in the fence, this bush is the only thing keeping it upright."

"They could plant something else. I don't think deadly nightshade is very neighbourly."

"They didn't plant it, Bonnie. They just haven't made much of an effort to uproot it. And I don't think they've felt that neighbourly since the day your father went round there to have a little word about the state of their dustbins."

I slammed the window shut. Sometimes I wonder what would happen to the world if everyone shared Constance's obsession with all the small potatoes of daily living. Would it grind to a halt? I had a sudden heart-uplifting vision of the vast, sleek and silver-bellied plane that would in only a few days lift me up and away, far from this great domestic compost heap of all my ancient marital failings. It was with the resolve and the fixed will of a man who sees freedom well within his sights that I sat down and, writing the words "Fifth Leamington Conference" in capitals as a subheading, set out to spin the very last bale of Fairbairn's fussy intellectual straw into pure, shining gold.

Rat-a-tat-tat!

It's her again. I'm going to murder her, so help me God.

"Go away, Constance! I am trying to work!"

"Olly, I need to tell you something. Now."

Since she's pre-empted the traditional response — "Can't it wait?" — I have to let her in.

"What is it this time?"

"Olly, don't be such a cross-patch. I wouldn't ask you if I didn't need your help."

"Can't you ask Ally?"

"No, of course I can't. He's coming with me. That's just the point. We are all going out."

Good.

"Really?"

"Yes. And you're to hold the fort when she turns up."

"Who?"

"Ratbag, of course."

"Stella? Why should she turn up here?"

"Because the day-care project closes down at four. And since by half-past she still wasn't there, the staff gave Ned to Ally. But when she finally shows up and finds the note that says he's with his father, she'll go mad. She'll be round here on her broomstick."

"But why can't —?"

Constance reads minds, you know, as well.

"Because we'll all be out. We're slipping away, quickly, over Stringbean's wall. We're taking Nance, Ned and Bonnie. It's up to you to man the barricades. When she arrives, tell her we'd no idea when she'd show up, so we've gone out for tea."

"Another tea? Where?"

She was already out of the room and halfway down the stairs.

"You're joking, Oliver! This woman is a killer. You're safer not knowing!"

"Constance —"

She'd gone. She was in such a hurry she'd even left her precious punnet sitting on top of my papers. I took it off, and had a little go at rubbing out the berry stains with a wet finger, till I thought better of it. Then I came downstairs too. If Constance thought that I was going to spend my afternoon placating Stella Ratbag, she was wrong. For all I cared, whole packs of outraged mothers could spend the afternoon milling around on the doorstep. I wouldn't let them in. The best plan for me was simply to make a pot of tea, then hole up in my attic till the crisis was over.

No need to spell it out, though. I acted casual as I filled the kettle. Constance was marching up and down the serried ranks of her expensive domestic appliances, switching off rumbles. Ned sat at the table, picking blackcurrants off the tart.

215

"Don't do that," Nancy scolded. "You'll leave holes."

Constance swung round as she heard Ally start up the getaway car.

"Money!"

She flew upstairs. Bonnie flew after her to fetch a woolly. Nancy trailed out to Ally, waiting in the car. And Little Ned, in mortal funk from going absent without leave, fiddled with all of the tea things still lying on the table till Constance and Bonnie rushed downstairs again.

"Quick, Ned."

"But I haven't filled in all the little —"

"Never mind that. Daddy is waiting." She swept him away from the table, and herded them all out of the back door. "Let's go the quick way, over Stringbean's wall."

She darted back one last time, to snatch the punnet off the table and hurl it in the bin. Then she was gone. I heard the desperate race of an engine in the lane. And then peace. Perfect, working peace. Merciful gods. I gathered everything on my tray, and carried it upstairs.

Rat-a-tat-tat!

Sorry. We're out.

Rat-a-tat-tat-tat-a-tat-tat-a-tat-tat!

Jesus! No wonder everyone's nerves are put on edge. But, sorry. No-one home.

RAT-A-TAT-A-TAT-A-TAT-A-TAT-TAT-TAT-TAT-TAT! THWACK! CRACK!

Constance was right. The woman was unhinged. Nevertheless, while she was flailing furiously on our front door it was impossible to concentrate, so I rose from my chair and edged towards the window. The noise

216

stopped suddenly, and I peeped out. Ratbag was standing in the garden now, with her back turned, and from the way she kept swooping down and poking about in the greenery, it was quite clear she had despaired of simple fisticuffs to get her way, and was now rooting down the verge of Ally's well-kept garden path, in search of a nice brick to batter the door down.

Constance went to some trouble with that paintwork. Knowing full well she would blame me for any mischief, I thought it best to take the more responsible line, and, sighing, I gave up and opened the window.

"Mrs —"

For a brief moment, Ally's second name escaped me. Then:

"Huggett! Mrs Huggett!"

She spun round. It was a moment or two before her furious peering found me out. But then she saw me leaning out of my window. Like a plain-clothes metropolitan police officer unmasked at a peaceful picket, she hastily dropped her brick, and stood, a vision on our garden path, making my heart go *thump*.

She was quite ravishing. Cross-eyed with temper, pink and panting with rage, but stunningly, stunningly lovely. Frankly, I look back now and I can't for the life of me make any sense of all that bilge from Constance about people thinking that Stella was jumble. The man in his right mind would buy her new. She was a dish, and when her silky summer skirt blew back against her body, it made me shudder in my shoes to think this ferocious little creature ever belonged to Cabbage Caliban. How did the two of them fit? How come she didn't break? His massive paws would —

"Can I help, Mrs Huggett?"

And what about in bed? How could this filigree fighter even breathe? How come the two of them produced young Ned? Surely not naturally! She wouldn't have lived! Ned must have been conceived by slim sterile dropper, not by Our He-Man of the Muddy Trowel, whose sturdy bonking sets the floorboards groaning two nights a week, and alternate Saturdays if Nance goes to Skates Club.

"Everyone else is out."

I nearly was, as well. If I leaned further I would catch a glimpse of where the top button of her flimsy bodice had somehow, gloriously, popped undone.

"I'll come straight down, shall I?"

I didn't wait for an answer. You could tell simply from the look on her face that, if she opened her mouth, she would spit toads. But, on the other hand, I couldn't very well leave her strutting about the front garden, prising up rocks to hurl at Constance's hard gloss. Wouldn't be fair. Safer to let her in. I could perhaps offer her a nice cup of tea, and a small strip of carpet to chew while she was waiting.

That was the big mistake. Constance was scornful enough about it afterwards. "I warned you, Olly. 'Man the barricades,' I said, not 'Open up the door and let her in.' You've read *Snow White*. Don't you learn *anything*? It serves you right!"

Served me right! How did she know? She wasn't even there. She'd slipped out quickly enough, over the back wall. She wasn't privileged to see me suffering the miseries of afternoon tea with Stella — who, I might

218

say, within moments of my handing out my deeply ill-advised invitation, broke clean through her barrier of speechless rage to demand instant access to the telephone, and to singe the wires with her malevolent and slanderous accusations. You'd think the poor women who run the play scheme had been blithely handing out other people's children, free of charge, to any homicidal maniac who happened to be strolling down Gosworthy Road round about closing time, the way Ratbag hurled abuse at them down the line.

"Don't be so foolish," I told her, when she hung up. "The man is Ned's father."

She turned to snarl at me.

"You can stay out of it!"

I set the tray down. I was about to show the woman the door, but seemingly inured to the effect her vile manner had on normal human beings, she'd scraped a chair back over Constance's new tiles and plonked herself down, the better to concentrate on further invective.

"What do you know about it? Nothing! You weren't married to that bastard. I was. And I can tell you that Alasdair Huggett is a cunning shit —"

Right then and there, I stopped listening. Constance was furious with me afterwards. "Surely you can remember what she said. Think, Olly. Think!" But it was hopeless. The moment the woman referred to Ally as a cunning shit, I pulled a mental plug. It is a habit and a very useful skill born of long years in academic seminars, when I was fool enough to feel obliged to sit politely while the intellectually lame came close to wasting whole afternoons of my life, filling the precious hours between two and four with all their ill-considered cerebral droppings. One stupid sentence, that is all it took. I'd almost wait for it. Then, reassured that the speaker had not wasted much of his own time thinking his topic through, I would no longer feel I must waste mine listening to his conclusions. I'd be away — still sitting watching him gravely, nodding sagaciously from time to time, and even smiling along with the others when I sensed the restless swell of a joke. But mentally I was as far gone as when, back then in nineteen hundred and frozen to death, Revilo Nesor lifted himself up and away from all the wringing claims, the endless bloodsucking demands, and took his rightful place as King of Mars.

And Ratbag's sentence was a give-away. "Alasdair Huggett is a cunning shit." It's a thin day for men when a huge healthy one of forty-two can fetch up like Ally — no house, no savings, income a joke (if it weren't pitiful), son under guard — and be A Cunning Shit. The woman's words were not worth space between the ears.

But watching her was quite another matter. I interrupted the vituperative flow just long enough to slip in one little word — "Tea?" — and, without faltering in her embittered stride, she stretched towards one of the cups. To my delight, her bodice cooperatively fell forward. Reaching a hand out, I cast about for the nearest chair and, pulling the thing towards me, sat down opposite. I couldn't peel my eyes off her.

"Sugar?"

She took a lot of sugar, for a sylph. And every spoonful she reached out to take was one more thrill for me. I realized suddenly I hadn't seen a woman (not counting my anaphrodisiac ex-wife) for nearly three whole months.

"Bit of blackcurrant tart?"

She didn't bother to knock off complaining about Ally long enough to say anything civil in the order of "Yes, please. That would be very nice. It looks delicious." But, living happily on hope, I cut a large slice for her anyway, and pushed it forward — not too far.

"Sprinkle of sugar on top?"

Again the little tuck and fall, the glimpse of pleasures so consistently denied through Fairbairn's fiendish summer. It was so long since I had let my mind stray down this track that the first stirrings of my own desire startled me physically.

"Cream?"

A calculated risk. I shunted Constance's revolting cow jug only one or two inches towards her. She really had to stretch. It was a joy. I sat back, satisfied, and watched her struggling with it. It's hard to pour. First none at all will come, then great mucous streams pour out of both its nostrils, and won't stop. She practically drowned her tart. But she didn't notice. Since she'd come through the door, I don't think she had really noticed anything, not even me watching the pale cream frothing on her lips, and basking thoroughly in her soft, swollen pleasures (and in mine). Constance was right. Nothing and no-one counted for anything with her, that was quite plain. She'd found a willing ear (albeit deaf), and no doubt if I had bothered to switch back on, I would have heard some twin in all but audience response of one of

Constance's brilliant Imitations of Ratbag, in which the selfish I's march through the soft Welsh lilt with the monotonous regularity of telegraph poles over flat countryside where there is nothing else, and no-one else, ever in view. Anyone listening would probably have felt a powerful urge to slug her. Me? I was entranced. I thought she was a stunner, a marvel, a glory. Eyes far, far bluer than blue. Hair fair as an angel basking in the sun. Glistening lips — oh, stop. Don't even think about it. Don't look back. I don't think I've ever seen a woman I've had so great an urge to take to bed. She had a body to make a man gently implode from sheer lust, a bodice that looked as if it would fall off her if she sneezed, and she was spoiling for a fight — with Ally, admittedly; but I did get the feeling it might be possible to nudge her off that very well-worn track, and, just this once, lure her into tangling with me.

I stuck her company for quite a while before I gave up hope. But the Trashing of Alasdair Huggett took all her attention. In fact, the longer she went on about her former hubby and the father of her child, the worse she seemed to get. She flushed. Her eyes went black. Even her breathing quickened. Constance said afterwards that these were the first symptoms, and I should have noticed the woman had begun to look a little odd, and act a little strangely; but as I rather tartly pointed out, how is one supposed to draw the very fine distinction between the behaviour of someone who arrives by charging up your garden path and beating your door down in a demented fashion, and someone who, flushed and croaking with what appears to be freshly stoked rage, suddenly charges away again? How is the layman supposed to notice the difference? I'm not a doctor, am I? Or a forensic pathologist. I never even noticed the little pockmarks that sprouted up all over Bonnie the weekend Constance went to France, till she and her mother came home on Sunday night and pointed them out. So how was I supposed to recognize the early subtleties of deadly-nightshade poisoning? Anyway, she'd eaten the buggers with lashings of good stomach lining. She'd really pigged out on the double cream, thanks to Constance's jug. So who's to say for sure it was the effect of the berries with which Ned had so dutifully refilled all the little damp holes in the pastry that sent the woman careering hysterically out of the door and down the garden path, straight under the wheels of that Volvo? It looked like pure temper to me. I said so then, and I maintain it now. Ned never poisoned her. She killed herself.

Mind you, all the assertions in the world won't halt the Inquisition when it starts. Constance was worse than the police.

"But, Olly, didn't you even notice that all the holes Ned had picked in the pastry had been filled up again?"

No. No, I didn't, Constance, as it happened. I was thinking about something else, I expect.

"But you were there, in the kitchen, making your pot of tea. Didn't you notice Ned picking berries out of the punnet you'd left on the table?"

No. No, I didn't, actually. Sorry. No.

"But, when you cut Stella a slice, didn't you even *notice* that those berries looked a little different in the tart — weren't even cooked?"

No. Again, I'm afraid to say it. I didn't notice. I didn't bloody notice! Just like I didn't notice Joe crying his eyes out at the garden gate, or Sol waving as he drowned, or Nancy swallowing that mothball, or any of the million or so other bloody things you'd have me fritter my time and mind away noticing, hour by hour, day by day, week by week, year by year, till my whole life's been chewed up to no obvious effect, just like your own. Well, bugger you, Constance. You ought to be grateful. You ought to be down on your knees thanking the gods that I don't notice little things like poisonous berries lurking in a tart. Don't think I didn't see the little look of hope that you exchanged with Alasdair when you lot finally came back and I had to tell you there'd been a bit of an accident. Oh, I know you looked suitably serious and anxious. But I also know that was because there were three children standing there watching and listening, one of them hers. I know you realized it was a lot more serious than I let on. And I did see that look.

So you owe me one, Constance. I have set you and Ally free, I've let Ned out of his cage. Don't think I haven't seen the change in him over the last few days. He is a different child. So don't play your Surely-You-Noticed-Oliver game with me about husky voices and abnormal thirst, flushed skin, fast breathing, incoherence, physical restlessness. You had as good as spent the summer telling me this sort of thing was just what you'd expect if you had Ratbag for tea. It's probably safe to say I wouldn't have thought twice about it if Stella had begun to froth at the mouth and chew the rugs. If I didn't guess that something was wrong, it's more your bloody fault than it is mine!

224

Not that I'm bitter. All the same to me. I must say I felt a little nervous once or twice while those policemen were sniffing round the place, asking their questions. But once it became clear even to that suspicious Detective Inspector Harris that every potential trail of black criminality led straight back to poor little freshly orphaned Ned and his attempts to hide his depredations on our blackcurrant tart, everyone seemed to back off. In fact, I got quite a lot of work done. Having to postpone the flight until after the inquest turned out to be a blessing in disguise. The delay did at least mean I managed to finish that bloody thing for Fairbairn down to the last footnote, and get it posted out of my life for good, even if having that argument with the lady at the post-office counter about what actually constitutes "a book" under her guidelines for cheap rates did make us a little bit late for the funeral.

Which I enjoyed. Ally gets anxious when I speak ill of the dead, but really the woman was corrosive by nature, and left an evil trail. I'm not surprised that there were only eleven people there, and it turned out to be such a merry occasion. It's not often Constance ends up inviting a whole load of perfect strangers (excluding Detective Inspector Harris, of course) back for a quick knees-up. The noise was tremendous. I could barely make out what Harris was going on about over the din that the children were making. But once it became clear it was no more than a puzzled professional's off-the-record action replay of everything I'd already had in spades from Constance ("But, Professor Rosen, if you don't mind my asking, didn't you even *notice* . . . ?")

I'm afraid that I rather stopped paying attention. I eavesdropped on a far more interesting conversation to my left, in which a rather charming young woman called Mandy (whose husband Ratbag had apparently made off with once) was suggesting that the extremely brief sighting of Stella's mother in the cemetery was to be explained, like her own presence, in terms of simply wanting to check on the exact position of the grave, so she could come back and dance on it later.

Anyway, they did all push off finally, at about a quarter to two. Ally and I carried the sleeping children up the stairs, and tipped them into their beds, while Constance took her time seeing Inspector Harris safely down the garden path. Then she and Ally dribbled off to bed. I came in here. I don't know if it was the noise of Ally's celebratory floor-groanings, or the champagne, that kept me from feeling sleepy. All I know is I took the opportunity to write a short postscript for Fairbairn (which I am sure he will refuse to print) about how Philosophy in Britain is now Dead, what with a whole generation wiped out by mindless governmental cuts, no books in the libraries and no time to think. Thank God I got away is all that I can say. (And no doubt did.)

And I'm not coming back — except, briefly, for the Sixth Leamington Conference, early next year. This place no longer even feels like home. I have moved on. Next time, the children can come out to me. The change will do them good. Bonnie can still remember the wonderful ice-cream parlours and the roller-skating rink, Nancy is jealous she can't, and pale little Ned could do with a few weeks of Prime Grade AA US beef, and some good West Coast sunshine. Anyway, Constance is going to need a little bit of peace now and again, if she is actually insane enough to go ahead with this new pregnancy. "Accident" indeed! I saw the proud and soppy look on Ally's face. His heart's desire is in his grasp at last. All of his precious eggs laid in one warm, cosy basket. Let's hope that Constance doesn't drop the lot. I wouldn't put it past her. I've been suspicious all along of all those heartfelt cries up the pipework: "Oh, Ally! Wouldn't it be wonderful if . . ."

If. It's a treacherous little brick for building castles in the air. Even professional philosophers treat "if" with care. God help the amateurs. And they are amateurs. "If it weren't for Olly . . ." "If it weren't for Ratbag . . ." What do the two of them suppose the future holds? Can they really believe they are going to be happy? Beware the message in the fortune cookie, Constance. Don't forget. "You can have what you want most in the world. You can't have what you wanted second and third." Choose to lean on a pit prop like Alasdair, and, after a bit, you'll notice that though your pit prop's big and strong and dependable, he's also made of wood. You'll get bored stiff. Right now the man might seem a good rest cure from me. But someone like you needs constant stimulation. I'd say that picking your way barefoot over the embers of marital dissatisfaction actually suited you, Constance, in a funny sort of way. It isn't in your nature to be content.

I hate to say it, but I suspect that this idyllic family nest will fall apart quite soon, without me and Ratbag. You needed her and me. Don't forget I've spent the whole of the last three months hearing the whispers up your pipes. I know what I'm talking about. Stella might have been an irritation, I might have got on your nerves a little, but at least we gave the two of you something to talk about. What will you chat about now? Giant hogweed? I prophesy some great long silences echoing upwards in the near future. And I know you, Constance. You'll go mad. You're not the sort to stick it. Someone like you always needs someone or something at which to chip away, day after day. I tell you, up until now Ratbag and I have been twin pillars of support. You two are on your own now. And it won't last.

Still. Not my problem. Tomorrow at noon, Oliver Rosen is flying out of here an unencumbered man. Well, only unencumbered because I finally managed to persuade you to ship the eight tons of boxes you had so very kindly gathered in the hall by international freight, instead of by air. God, what a harridan you can be. Ally is welcome to you. You should have seen yourself yesterday, standing arms akimbo in the hall. "I'm sending everything this time, Oliver. I warn you. Everything. All the music. Everything festering in those old trunks. The whole lot. I don't care what it costs, I'm not keeping any of it any longer. Ned has to move up to the attic so that the baby can be next to us. You have to take your stuff — every last sheet of paper — and I mean it!"

Good job you haven't seen this lot. You'd go berserk. There's more of this than there was of all that stuff for Fairbairn. I've had to move into another pillowcase. I can't take all this with me on the flight. It's far too heavy. It needs typing up.

I'll leave it here. Stuff silly, simpering Victoria Plum and her pastel pals down further at the back, where you won't find them. Where I hope you won't find them. I know you. One finger on this lot, and the first time I have the temerity to hint at a slight pruning of your princely allowance, you'll probably gather the whole pile together and bloody publish it. I wouldn't put it past you. You wouldn't care. You've never had the slightest sense of privacy. I've said so all along. And, knowing your luck, you'll probably make a lot more money out of publishing this than I made out of old Fairbairn.

Oh, never mind. When you come down to it, it's that or having one more bloody row about bunging up your closets. I couldn't stand it. I am going *home*.

Finished? Sure? Quite sure you don't want to fly back for a day or two, and add another paragraph of complaints about my failings as a wife, or Ally's as a breadwinner? Sure you don't want to put a curse on anyone else's future happiness while you're at it? My mother's? The children's? You've written enough, have you, Olly?

Right. Pass the phone. You're dead right this will make a heap more loot than all that dreary stuff you spent the summer churning out. And I don't just want a Steinway. I want a holiday in France, a new car, and some designer pregnancy frocks, and a new ten-speed bike. And Alasdair needs a new mower. And Bonnie needs shoes. And . . . and . . . and . . . and . . .

And Oliver, you *must* have known that I would come across it. I do change sheets! This lot was far too big to hide. You've covered reams. Why, in type, it must be safely two hundred pages.

Mind you, it is a very well-known fact that autobiographies are much, much easier to write than Truth. You go ask Bertrand Russell.

And easier to find. Ask Victoria Plum.

THE END